MW00565027

The
Disillusioned

THE 'NAM' ... FROM BOTH SIDES

John W. Conroy

Cover design KC Reiter
Cover photos John W Conroy

Press information conroyvn@gmail.com
1 518 572 5962

Screenplay available

Viet Nam 1975

Design by KC Reiter

GLOSSARY

APC - Armored Personnel Carrier

CIA - Central Intelligence Agency

MACV - Military Assistance Command Vietnam

USARV - U S Army Republic Vietnam

ARVN - Army Republic Viet Nam (southern)

VNAF - Viet Nam Air Force (southern)

NVA - North Vietnamese Army

PAVN - Peoples Army of Viet Nam (northern)

1ST CAV - US Army First Cavalry Division

NLF - National Liberation Front (southern)

VC - Viet Cong

IVS - International Voluntary Services

bo doi - NVA foot soldier

NGO - Non Governmental Organization

LZ - Landing Zone

P - Piastre

GI - US Army Foot Solder

LT - Lieutenant

BOQ - Bachelor Officer Quarters

SGN - Airport ID for Saigon

GREEN MACHINE - The US Army

MI - Military Intelligence

HUEY - All Purpose US Army Helicopter

K – KILOMETER

"If I believed in your God in another life, I'd bet my future harp against your golden crown that in five hundred years there may be no New York or London, but they'll be growing paddy in these fields, they'll be carrying their produce to market on long poles wearing their pointed hats. The small boys will be sitting on the buffalos......"

Graham Greene

TABLE OF CONTENTS

CHAPTER 1:

THE RETURN

EARLIER TODAY, I FLEW INTO HANOI ON AN AIR FRANCE from Paris. As the plane begins its approach, I look out the window on a sea of green, the Viet Nam I knew from years past, and I begin thinking of those days. The later ones, near the end of that dirty war. At that time my best friend was Jake Barns, a Major who flew Helicopter Support for the ARVN troops that I was attached to as an advisor. It was my third tour in Viet Nam, and I was a bit long in the tooth for that game. My first tours were over by mid-1966 and I returned to Port Kent on Lake Champlain in northern New York State where my forbears were from, and where I'd spent summers as a youth. After eventually opting for more education and finishing law school I set up practice in the small village of Keeseville, a short distance inland from the hamlet of Port Kent.

However, the Viet Nam gig was a war without end and memories of that time stayed forefront in my mind. I wasn't able to concentrate on local law....so much trivial nonsense it seemed to me at that time.

So, I went back. Same old rank of Captain and since most of the American GIs had long left the country, I found myself living and working with the ARVN Marine Division, functioning as their US advisor and Air Liaison Officer with what little US air support was available. We operated in a good part of I Corps with headquarters in Da Nang.

Major Jake Barns was very often the pilot who landed his Huey with supplies and reinforcements. At the same time, in most cases he was the sole medivac available to ferry the wounded back to triage. Jake was also my cousin….a few times removed. His family lived a short distance down the lake from Port Kent at Chimney Point in Vermont. Years ago, and for the better part of a century his people built clocks, and they were famous for it. Jake however chose another line of work. After attending Norwich on a ROTC scholarship, he ended up in army aviation and was well on his way to being a lifer.

The one mystery of that time was my captor, a Sgt. Chanh. For a short time as Da Nang was falling, he had me. I'd passed on the World Airways 727, the last flight from Da Nang to Saigon and consequently ended up a prisoner of the NVA under the supervision of Sgt. Chanh who commanded a platoon of infantry. I guess what saved me was my ability to speak Vietnamese at which I was not particularly good, but it proved to be adequate. After all, it more than likely saved my life for in those last hours of the war life was cheap, and it was getting cheaper by the minute. I grew to like Sgt Chanh and we talked endlessly, long into the night. We were both in the same boat…tired like hell of war. It was time for all of us to go home.

At any rate, all the old memories were now on hold. I left my room at the Metropole Hotel, supposedly the best in Hanoi, and was on my way to the US Embassy to visit another old friend from those days gone by in Da Nang. Wales Signor had been a foreign service officer at the Da Nang consulate when I knew him during that time. He is now the Ambassador from the US to Viet Nam, and I am greatly looking forward to a meeting with him. We had several years to catch up on. We'd not seen each other since just before Da Nang fell on that fateful Easter Sunday in 1975. After walking around Hoan Kiem Lake, all the time keeping my eye open for the sacred giant turtle of legend, I grabbed a cab for the short ride to the newly opened US Embassy on Lang Ha St. I am eventually granted entry and directed to a waiting room where in due time the ambassador shows up.

"Well, I'll be damned, if it isn't Captain Edward Winslow, the last white man out of Da Nang, and that was after it fell. Ed, how the hell are you?" said Ambassador Signor.

"Well from the looks of your digs here I'm not keeping up with you, but I'm ok. Still at it. Who the hell ever could have thought we'd meet up here in Hanoi? Pretty weird...but maybe it's fate."

"Whatever it is Ed it is, but it's great to see you again. Look, I'm going to be tied up here for the better part of the day. How about meeting up at the Metropole bar for happy hour 5:30 or so. I should be good to go for the evening.

"Good enough Wales. I'll be there. I'm staying there actually. Think I'll spend the day wandering around town. Everything here is all new to me.... and very unexpected."

"You'll want to go to the Ho Chi Minh mausoleum and there's also a great war museum you'd probably like. Perhaps. We're not shown to be the heroes up here... if you get my drift. See you at the Metropole, Ed."

I did stop in at the mausoleum and the museum but was impressed by neither. I have seen it all and read too much to give a damn anymore. I'm up here for one reason. To see if I can find Hoa, my late wife Lien's sister.

It's been a couple of years now and I still miss Lien terribly. She was my soul mate many months before Da Nang fell and remained so throughout the years. We had been living in Australia for all our life together after leaving Viet Nam in 1975. We ran a restaurant, and we ran a farm, and it worked until the cancer showed its face. So... after wandering the world since her death I end up here, not exactly where it all began, but close enough. Even one old friend in the same town. Who knows if I can even find the sister Hoa or what would happen if I did, but this search gives me a mission, and that's good enough for now.

One thing about bars in Viet Nam, there are always beautiful girls working behind and in front of the bar, so one never lacks for conversation with a knockout beauty…and that's a good thing.

"What your name GI. My name Mai."

I looked up from my gin and tonic and said to myself 'what the hell'.

"Just kidding with you mister, but you do look like an old soldier to me. You can see that I'm much too young to have known a real one, from America that is. You are an American, aren't you?"

"Certainly, but you threw me off with the old GI lingo. For a moment I thought I was back in time. How do you happen to speak such correct English, Mai?"

"School. What do you think? I'm an English major and a graduate of Da Nang University. I work full time up here for the American company Morrison-Knudson. In fact, I run their office."

"Good for you, but how do you happen to be working this bar, if I may ask?"

"It be my night job." Then she laughed a beautiful laugh. "Just kidding Mister…what is your name?"

"It be Edward." Then we both laughed like hell, and I was beginning to like this place, and that's how the conversation continued until Wales showed up.

"I see you've met the beautiful Mai" he said as he mounted the stool beside me. We continue along these lines before getting down to basics and catching up on our lives over the last twenty some odd years. It turns out that Wales has been working steady with the Foreign Service. He'd worked his way up to the ambassador level earlier with a posting in El Salvador but picked this plum position here when the embargo ended, and full diplomatic relations were restored. His earlier experience at the consulate in Da Nang had been great background as well as his command of the language. He was riding higher than myself, but I for one did not care about that kind of thing any longer.

Wales continued with "it's tricky here though. Both sides are learning how to deal with each other. Let's face it, we have a horrific past with the Vietnamese to contend with and the tendency for us has been to just ignore it. I might add they find that hard to accept but are doing their best. Pragmatism is among their great traits. I mean, hell, they need our business and their entre into the world economy is greatly facilitated by cooperating with us."

In my own way I was overly familiar with everything he was talking about and was more interested in the personal side of our past over the last number of years. He mentioned that he was married to a woman from an old Virginia family by the name of Westmoreland.

"Don't tell me you married one of his fucking cousins," I burst out with. "You had such an eye for the local girls back in Da Nang that I figured you'd end up with one. There're a lot of lookers from Viet Nam living in the Washington area."

"You're right about that Ed but things worked out otherwise. I met Cornelia at a Department function and that was that. And she is his distant cousin, but I couldn't hold that against her. After all, she was a wild one in bed. We have one daughter who is a freshman at Vassar so I'm here alone for now. Corn wanted to stay in the States till Lou Anne is settled in. Meanwhile, I do keep an eye out here…Mai for instance. Let's face it, Corn and I were married later than most and at the moment she's an old white woman. Still quite nice looking, very pleasant, but still…an old white woman. And Mai is a young, beautiful, brilliant… girl let's say. Who can resist?"

I'm thinking there's no end to it. There was a book by an old state department hand from the fifties and early sixties who lived in Saigon during that time. It was his opinion that the main reason that we were staying in Vietnam was the women. If they weren't what they were we'd have left years ago…because of the heat if nothing else. There wasn't really a legitimate point for being here. This time it seems like we're back at the beginning, and in many ways we are.

My intention is to catch Wales up with my life in Australia with Lien. He had flown with her to Saigon on one of the last planes from the Marble Mountain Air Strip, when my fate was unknown to them as Da Nang was falling. They had separated on landing in Saigon and she and I eventually, very luckily, met up in the Aussie bar, the Kangaroo, where our old friend John Sanderson had Australian visas prepared for us. Life had been so rushed and complicated for the next couple of years that I lost contact with my Viet Nam people.

"You know " said Wales, "I wasn't all that hopeful Lien would ever see you again. On arrival at Tan Son Nhut, we caught a cab for the Embassy and quickly went our separate ways. For all I knew you were dead on the runway at the Da Nang Airport. We heard all about that catastrophe of the World Airways 727 on the ramp and on the trip south. And aside from a few rumors, I knew nothing of either of you till earlier today when you showed up at the Embassy."

"Seems like we both got on with our lives a half a world away from each other. We were a lot luckier than most who were trying to leave town that day."

"You're right on about that old boy," he said. Then, " Mai could you get us another round of drinks please."

I ignored her smile, which was directed at Wales anyhow, and filled him in on my life with Lien in Australia. We had lived a very normal life, especially since our existence together before that had been anything but normal. We ran a small farm; a kind of subsistence farm a short distance outside of Sydney for a few years and then began a restaurant using our produce from the farm. That kind of thing was just catching on in those days and we were quite successful. It didn't hurt that I ended up with a PTSD pension from the VA. In the end Viet Nam had paid off, both financially and romantically.

But nothing lasts forever. Three years ago, Lien contracted breast cancer. The diagnosis was late, and she lived less than a year. I was devasted and eventually sold out everything we had amassed together in Australia. I just wandered the world for a couple of years, then returned to Port Kent for a visit with relatives and began thinking about Viet Nam once again. Lien had spoken often of her sister Hoa but had made no attempt to visit. For whatever reason they lost contact. Nothing was easy about Viet Nam during the years of the US embargo.

"So you see Wales, here I am. Once again drinking with you in Viet Nam in the company of a beautiful woman. I like being back 'in country' but the real reason I've showed up is to contact Lien's sister Le Thi Hoa. I've often thought it's too bad Omar isn't around. He could find anyone, anywhere in Viet Nam."

Wales mentioned that he had known Omar faintly while living in Da Nang, but he didn't run in the same company that Barns and I did. Omar was one of our main men. He had been ready to pack in the war for some time but hadn't been able to. Viet Nam was his home, and the deal was the same as the guys on the other side. 'Fight till we win…or die trying'. He'd been with the 199th Light Infantry Brigade in Bien Hoa, for a time working as their interpreter. After the Tet Offensive he eventually ended up in Da Nang, rather like Barns and me. His English was so good that he continued working as an interpreter, mostly for communication with the little American air support that remained in country assisting various ARVN units. I hoped he made it, and knowing him, he did.

"To get back to Hoa Ed, I have heard of her. She's a journalist that does not maintain good relations with the government. I guess you'd call her a progressive and heaven knows that there is plenty this government could learn to be progressive about."

He then proceeded to fill me in on some background on Hoa.

'The strange thing is I never knew of any connection between this rebel journalist and your Lien. Of course, why would I? She must have a place somewhere in Hanoi, though I do know that she's originally from Thai Nguyen, a fairly large town some ways north of here. Beyond that you'd have to start digging but knowing this country you'll turn her up in no time in Thai Nguyen. Find yourself a driver that'll head up there and go for it. Any trouble, give me a call."

It took some doing but this morning I finally made arrangements with an old driver my age to head north. His name was Quan and he too had been in the war and fought in the A Shau valley around the same time I had. His conversation was not what I expected. Nothing like the 'great patriotic war' that Russian soldiers espoused when speaking of their past glory. This guy was pissed off.

"I spent ten years in the army fighting you people" said Quan, "most of that time deep in the jungle. Sick, no food, sometimes even not much ammunition. I wanted to go home to my village, find a wife, have some kids and just grow rice. Fuck the war. The memory of it makes me sick."

He drove along in silence for a spell after that outburst. Oddly enough I have to say that I agreed with him. While I was a long way short of ten years in the field, I'd been there long enough to become completely disillusioned with the whole operation. Thinking back, my captor Sgt. Chanh's opinions differed little from driver Quan. Who wants to grow old killing people, and trying to avoid being killed yourself? Who wants to lose their youth to a battlefield?

I began talking with him about my life since the war years. He took an interest and perked up when I mentioned Le Thi Hoa being my wife's sister. He was sure he could locate her for he had a couple of old friends from the war who lived in Thai Nguyen and like everywhere in Viet Nam, 'everyone knows everything about everyone' or so they all think. We rode along at peace for a spell enjoying the view of the countryside. I noticed the hills that the Americans called 'thud ridge' during the war but considered keeping quiet on that topic. 'Thuds' were F-105 Thunderchiefs that used these hills for a fix on their bombing runs into Hanoi from Thailand. But he was ahead of me.

"Those hills be Thud Ridge," said Quan. "You know what that is"?

I really didn't want to get into a pissing match about an old war but admitted that I indeed did know what that was. He let it go, which surprised me. Perhaps we were both like a number of old warriors…just let the fucking thing go.

Thai Nguyen isn't such a large town. It reminded me of Bien Hoa during the war. About that size which is big enough for a town. Quan stopped at a coffee shop where it soon became apparent, he was pals with the old guy running it, so we sat for coffee and began typical coffee shop conversation… Vietnamese style. Which may have been the best way for me to locate Lien's sister Hoa. They hemmed and hawed….they talked about the weather…. they looked lasciviously at two young girls sitting alone in the corner…they joked between themselves.

"What about it Quan…can we get down to business? It's a long way back to Hanoi."

He eventually did get into the subject at hand and in no time had an address. After driving around for a bit, jabbering with people along the street, he pulled up to a house on the outer fringe of town. This area was essentially a country village and the house I was directed to was just a small cottage.

A remarkedly attractive woman answered the door and after looking at me for a moment said…in English "you must be Ed, my long-lost brother?"

I was surprised by the English and even more so because she recognized who I was even though we had never met. I answered "yes, I am, and you of course are Hoa…my long lost sister." This produced a smile from her, a low key smile.

She fixed tea and after taking seats on an outside veranda overlooking a beautiful garden that was predominantly vegetable, we began telling each other our very different stories of years gone by, and that long ago war; where the sisters were separated and I as an older man was lucky enough to have met the beautiful Lien. I was curious though of Hoa's great command of the English language.

"Well, you see I began work as a journalist during the war and eventually was able to have a few pieces printed in the international press. That was mostly in French papers in the beginning, and I knew French well from school, but the time came that I realized that if I wanted to get anywhere beyond 'local' and France is local for us up here, I'd have to learn English. I admit it took me a few years, but I had the time as I wasn't going anywhere at that point."

She spoke of a lover that was sent away to fight in the south in the late Sixties and on his one visit home she became pregnant.

"I had a child to raise by the time the war ended. His father never returned. We were unable to find out what became of him."

I told her how sorry I was to hear that and was hoping that her son had grown up healthy and was doing well today.

"Anh is doing very well" she said. "He teaches school and has given me two grandchildren, so I have nothing to complain about these days."

"I have a friend at the American Embassy in Hanoi, and he mentioned that you have had some trouble with the government over the years. What's that about?"

"I'm sure you're aware the government here is somewhat restrictive, to say the least, on opinions made public that do not agree with government policy. I'm a journalist and write the truth. Sometimes that doesn't jive with their view. So, what have you? I don't really give a damn anymore."

"I see you're up on English colloquialisms" I said... and she smiled.

I'd always wondered how it happened that Lien had ended up in Da Nang. She was always vague on that topic for some reason and during all those years living together it never mattered. We had other real-world problems. And also, we had remained very active lovers till the end of her life, so I figured why the hell stir things up digging into her past. But I did ask Hoa.

"I'll tell you something, my brother Edward. You were born out in the world. Lien and I were not. You cannot really imagine what life was like here on the outskirts of Thai Nguyen. Our world had perhaps a circumference of less than 10 Kilometers. Growing up we had never been farther than that. Nor had my mother. Father fought the French. He was wounded at Dien Bien Phu, and after returning grew rice for the rest of his life, and never again left our two-hectare farm".

She is quiet for a moment then leaves to prepare more tea. And I began thinking. Where I grew up, as Hoa just stated, the whole world was available. My parents were professionals in Albany where life was easy, and I spent summers up north on the lake. You couldn't beat it. We even had beautiful, brilliant cousins from London who visited for some of those summers. They were female cousins. We had schools, we had travel; we were a universe removed from a village in Viet Nam.

"Here's more hot tea if you would like some," said Hoa. She filled my glass and continued her story of two young girls.

"Lien was always more adventurous than I. She was restless to get going, but there was nowhere to go up here. My mother made arrangements for Lien to go live with her brother, our uncle. He had moved to Da Nang before the division was made permanent in 1956."

I interrupted her to inquire how that happened since the border between North and South had been closed permanently years before Lien had moved in with her uncle.

"There wasn't much" she said, "but some movement was still possible, even after the Americans landed in force on Red Beach in Da Nang. I don't remember all the details exactly but obviously she made it. After that there was only the rare letter. Even mail was difficult after the Americans took over. We lost touch over the years. There was only that one short note saying how she had married an American named Edward Winslow."

We spent the rest of the afternoon drinking tea and talking, getting to know each other. It was well after dark before Quan and I arrived back in Hanoi.

CHAPTER 2:

———————————

DA NANG 1974

I'M WALKING DOWN ALONG THE WATERFRONT OF THE HAN River close to where the fishing fleet operating out of Da Nang is anchored. The boats are a little ragged but painted a beautiful hue of blue with red eyes on the bow. Mixed among them and tied up along the docks are smaller American motorized craft along with barges of varying sizes. The Bamboo Bar, my destination, is perhaps half a klick farther down the street, and even though it's early for the evening crowd, I figured to sit alone on the deck that faced the river and enjoy the peace and quiet.

The temperature is just about perfect, and the skies are clear. The beautiful Van Ly serves me a cold 33, and Omar walks in. He's been working as an interpreter for the ARVN Marine Division commanded by Major General Bui Lan, a real tough bastard. Sgt. Omar has been fighting this war with various US and ARVN units for nearly ten years.

"How's it going Sarge? Looks like a slow night down here along the river."

"That be ok. I do not like fighting any more. You get my drift my Captain"?

"On that point Omar we, among many others, are in complete agreement. We pretty much see eye to eye, don't we?" Van Ly very soon delivers another 33 for Omar.

We sat there for some time without either of us speaking. Sometimes... what's the point? Neither he nor I can change a damn thing in this town. This war has a life of it is own and it goes on and on with men dying on both sides. Actually, not much has changed up here in I Corps for a couple of years. Mind you there are rumors that things might break wide open sooner than later. The North has held land below the DMZ since 1972 but the lines have been flexible. So, who knows? Omar orders another round and begins.

"I wonder what I'll be doing when this all be over Capt. I mean fuck it man, how are things going to end up? I have to remain here along with my family."

"Omar, it doesn't do any good to think that far ahead. Don't you remember the days when we were young, and we thought beyond nothing but the next evening. Some beer or some wine or maybe even whiskey...but mostly about finding ourselves in the arms of a young beauty. There wasn't a hell of a lot more that mattered back then."

"Easy for you to say Captain Winslow. Your family is safe back in the States. Mine be in Saigon, a risky place to be these times."

Conversation continues along those lines, mixed in with periods of silence. In many ways we were talked out. I'm hoping that Lien will stop in. We're living together on Tran Phu St., one up from the river. On some nights I have to maintain a presence at my station with the ARVN Airborne who are posted at the Air Base that is still managed by the United States Air Force. I'd spent last night alone in my hooch and had been missing her.

"Well, you could say Omar, that I have a similar problem these times right up here in Da Nang. I'd like to spend the rest of my life with Lien, but I don't think it's going to be here in 'God's Country'. I'm not joking. I've learned to love your country, but it might be many years before we from the States are allowed back in. I don't delude myself. As a country we're going to have a hell of a lot to answer for by the time they drive us out."

"You think that's a problem for you. How do you think I'm going to make it? I work ten years for the army who destroy us. They be calling us collaborators, like in France after the big war. What happen to them?"

That stumped me for a moment for I haven't been looking at it that way…however he isn't off base.

"You ought to have a month or so to make it back to Saigon by the time Da Nang falls and I'm sure a clever guy like yourself can figure something out".

"Easy for you to say, one more time Captain Winslow. Forgive me sir, but I do not think so highly of your country even though I fight with you. I know people. Like us, yours will look out for their own before they give a little Sargent like myself a ticket to paradise…not to mention my wife and kids".

I called for Van Ly and ordered another round of beers, hoping that there might be a way out for both of us. I mean, hell, we're Americans. Omar is almost one too. Van Ly sits down with us as she delivers the 33s.

"I listen to your conversation Captain Edward and you too Omar and I think maybe I might have same problem. I work for GI customer many years now. Since I twelve years old I sell coke and many other things along the road to passing GI. Everybody I know work for GI. They have all the money. What you think Captain"?

"All I can say to both of you, and even to myself is that undoubtedly there will be problems along the line that you both speak of. We'll have to try and figure it out."

My worry is Lien, for she has papers for nowhere but this South Vietnam and there is a good possibility that this country might just up and disappear. Anything is possible and I suppose that's the truth of the matter in any damn war. I hear English being spoken in the bar. Then out on the deck walked Jake Barns with his crew chief/door gunner, Spec. 5 Bobby D Banks on his who knows how many tours in this crazy country.

"Get ready for this one Ed" said Jake Barns, "we flew Dust Off for the ARVN 5th Rangers a little after noon and just got in. As you can imagine it was a clusterfuck. Like almost always, bad intel. The Rangers were scouting an area up by Tra My that should have been clear of NVA. People up in the foothills had reported that things were quiet, not any local VC around either. In fact, it was too quiet, so the outlook was that they dropped back towards the Trail on the Laotian border."

"Ok Barns, but what the hell happened"? .

"Listen cousin, give me time. There must have been some NVA doing the same kind of scouting that our men were attempting who were out-numbered and pinned down. There was no air support or artillery for some fucking reason, and they lost two. Three more were wounded by the time we slipped in with door gunners working overtime. A hotter than hell LZ I'll have you know. Right Banks?"

"Hotter than this redneck from Arkansas ever wants to see again. Van Ly, how about a whiskey coke for me, a big one. Maybe two. I can't seem to settle down. Don't know what the hell's wrong."

"Well," I say. "This is my third tour. Barns and Banks can't remember how many they've pulled. Omar, you're pushing ten years in the field. Van Ly, you have grown up in the midst of it. Boys and girls, it is time to wrap up this operation before one of us gets nailed. So on with it, whatever that means. How about another round Van Ly…and two for yourself?"

We four soldiers sit together quietly for a spell, saying little. The reality is each of us is powerless to have any effect on this war period. I came back here because it did seem to have a life of its own and I couldn't stay away. Now I wonder why the hell I am here. Lien and I wouldn't be a couple if I'd stayed in Keeseville, that's for sure but I'm beginning to question my judgement. I'll have to keep my eyes open and ears alert.

"I've heard that your unit might need some helicopter support for an insert in a day or two. How about it Omar? Or you Ed, am I going to be working with your unit?" says Maj. Barns.

"Who can know? " replied Omar. "We lose officers last week and be short on command people. If we know in the morning, we be lucky."

"He's right Jake. We operate in the grey. They'll play it by ear in the morning and we'll know early enough. Don't we always. Just have your bird ready, right Banks?"

"It is… now at this moment. If they need us in the morning let's hit it then. Right now, I need another whiskey coke."

I pick up one more round then leave for our pad on Tran Phu St. hoping that Lien will be home. In the morning I'll hook up with Barns along with the C O and get a handle on the day's operation. On entering our place, I notice that Lien was lying in bed reading a letter. It was from her mother and was the first she's received since I met her.

"Hey, how are you my one true love, Winslow" she says as I walk in.

I'm used to it but for some it always seemed strange that most of us are known by our last names among the locals, especially the girls and often, even after we had formed intimate relationships. If you think of it name tags on uniforms are last names and that's how everyone referenced everyone, and the girls know no difference. First names might come about after a period of time, but the surname remains.

"I was looking for you Lien and hoping that you were here in our little love nest."

"You see that a letter has come for me. It was written almost a year ago and is the first word I've had from my family in the North since much longer. The war makes that. For Vietnamese family is everything but my mother and myself have not even spoken through a letter in way over a year. That be number ten, GI."

I think she is trying to inject humor into her rather sad predicament, for we have moved much beyond bar girl-GI lingo. I sit down on the bed and hug her and notice tears in her eyes. She speaks softly of her sister Hoa. They had been inseparable as kids but now have lost touch.

"Maybe it is because we are young, and each have our own lives in different countries, that even being so close, are really a world away. Someday when this war ends, if it ever does, we can be people again. Like regular people who work their fields and talk with their friends and have meals with family and are friends with the young of their family and the whole village laughs and just lives together. I remember when that was the way it was…a long time ago."

I am quiet after that and curl up with her on the bed under the fan and we both drift off in a fitful slumber. There is no need to speak of when the war ends, for we don't know any more than the generals and the presidents… only that it does not bode well. We live for another day, hoping for the best.

CHAPTER 3:

THE OPERATION

THE NEXT DAY ARRIVES IN FULL FORCE. I LEFT LIEN SLEEP-
ing leaving much before sunrise so that I could stay ahead of the curve with
my ARVN s. Coffee went well with Barns early in the mess hall before the
rush of government soldiers. They are trying; however it appears to me that
the fatigue and despair that is going through my mind is spreading. It isn't me
that is affecting them for I am insignificant, a foreigner in their midst who is
tolerated but doesn't belong. There is a feeling of malaise which emanates from
somewhere within. It's in the air.

At any rate the word came in that three Hueys, Barn's among them, will be
used for an insert in the vicinity of the A Shau Valley by mid-morning. This ought
to work out. Barns flying his chopper with me in the back with the marines. Omar
following in one of the other two, manned by Vietnamese pilots and gunners.

And it came to be. Before noon the three machines were enroute, loaded
with ARVN Marines flying towards an insert on the western edge of the A Shau
near the Laotian border. Omar is following Barns but by not much. A Super
Sabre is visible diving on a target somewhere among the terraced crop land that
is surrounded by mountainous jungle.

We are closing in, but throttle back, not knowing the extent of the range that the F-100 is bombing. Barns has his Huey in a near hover. Suddenly two F-4 Phantoms fly overhead, diving just beyond us, dropping their bomb loads which includes canisters of napalm. Then they too climb out and head for home. And it looks like we are next.

I'm wearing a helmet that's plugged into the radio net as are the pilots and gunners. We'd had a general plan but were not expecting this kind of air support and had no idea what to anticipate on landing. Then one of the Phantom's reported in on our net. Better later than never I suppose.

"We are not sure of our targets," said the pilot. "A call came in from a LURP team. Ours, not the gooks. We lost contact and were bombing in the vicinity of the fix that was radioed to us by them. I hope they used good judgement and were well clear because there's nothing left alive down there now, not after that last pass. Low on fuel and leaving Dodge. See you back in Da Nang."

Then Maj. Jake Barnes chimes in with "What now Ed. Who's running this show?"

I spoke quicky with the ARVN Marine Captain who was in charge of this patrol. It was apparent that he was doubtful ... confused if you will. but said, "tell the pilot to land on the fringe of the Air Force targets if there is little ground fire. If LZ hot, no can do. Back to Da Nang."

I really couldn't blame the guy, why die here. I felt the same way myself, and so did Barns. He'd been wanting to leave for the last six months to take a flying job servicing the oil platforms in the seas surrounding Indonesia. The hell with being a lifer.

The captain said, " take it in Major. If the fire is excessive, call it off and back to base... and we live to fight another day."

"Roger" said Barns. "Tell the boys to hang on to their asses."

"Let's not lose sight of the fact that some of our boys are down there," I chimed in with. "They deserve some help,".

I mean fuck it, there's no one else but us, we've got to go in. Fire was light so with door gunners blazing away we were able to land close to the tree line. I remained in the machine behind the gunner as the Marines disembarked. The opposition fighters apparently melted into the landscape. as no fire was returned. In short order I leaped out, mostly so the troops would make a thorough search of the area for the LURP team which was my main reason for being on the ground. No need to call in more air support. The tree line bordered a large area of the valley that was covered with tall grasses; very beautiful…and very deadly. Substantial areas had been laid bare by napalm

The two Hueys that had been following us in had landed nearby so a thorough search of the bombed area was possible in short order. As I trailed along after my platoon of marines a commotion began up front. One of the troops began yelling so fast I wasn't able to understand him at first. Then it was apparent. Bodies…or rather parts of bodies. Omar showed up before I was able to make a close inspection…but when I did. They were ours. Son of a bitching bastard. These poor kids.

"I think friendly fire from jet plane Captain," said Omar. "No way NVA can do this damage. Very bad… very, very bad."

"Omar, take some men a distance from the area to be sure no snipers are left behind. I'll gather up any identifying info if anything's left. "

LURP teams often went in 'black ops' if cross border activity was in the works so nothing in the way of ID would be on them. It looked that way here. I was able to have the ARVN Marines that had not left with Omar grab some body bags from the choppers and begin the gruesome task of picking up the pieces. The old expression of bag 'em and tag 'em wouldn't apply here since there was no real way of knowing the total number of bodies.

Omar's squad did find a couple of NVA corpses that had been left behind. They too were loaded on the Huey for closer inspection back in Da Nang. Army Intelligence would give them a thorough going over back at triage. We flew home in silence. Neither Barns nor I were in the mood for conversation….perhaps tonight at the Bamboo.

CHAPTER 4:

AU SHAU VALLEY

A SOLDIER IN THE UNIFORM OF THE PEOPLE'S ARMY OF Viet Nam (PAVN) is lying on a hill overlooking a lush, green valley. It's a beautiful day with a bright sun high in the sky. He's lying back enjoying himself, the peacefulness, the absence of his army. Silence, but for the chirping of an occasional bird. Sgt. Chanh has been fighting in the South of Viet Nam for nearly ten years. He's sick of it. He wants to go home. His thoughts drift back to the beginning of it all, his home village of Tan Lap.

He remembers the enthusiasm of those times when all the young men, or perhaps just old boys, left for the South to defend their country from US Imperialism. None of them had any idea what that meant but there was a history of men from the village leaving a generation earlier to fight the French, and before that the Japanese. Chanh's mind drifted back to earlier days. Back to the years of his youth when he was with his friends in the rice fields and frog ponds of the countryside of Tam Lap. Some had already been killed in the war. Bao and Vinh were among those who had passed on to the great beyond. They had been wiped out by B-52s while on the Ho Chi Minh

Trail before ever making it to battle. That's the kind of war this was….a dirty fucking war.

Vinh loved frogs. He kept them for pets. Chanh and Bao loved frogs too…their legs that is. They loved eating them…but not Vinh. He wouldn't kill a living thing. There were ducks in those fields and water buffalo to be ridden and tended too. The work went along with the play or perhaps the work was play. That's how it was growing up on a farm in Viet Nam when Chanh was young.

The rumble of bombs is heard in the distance, and it draws Chanh from dreams of his childhood. He looks out over the valley as an American Phantom jet quickly descends to drop bombs then climbs out nearly over his position. His mind quickly shifts from the past of his youth to the absolute present.

He stands up for a better view down the valley. There could be soldiers from his unit down there below the bombs. He feels guilty for a moment then appreciates the fact that he's immeasurably lucky. Survival under the armaments of these jet fighters is one hundred percent luck. You could do nothing to make a difference but burrow into the ground somehow and bury yourself. Even then it was still nothing. Just look at the craters that were left behind. More than enough to bury his whole unit.

"I wonder" Chanh is thinking. "This war was sold to us as a great patriotic struggle. But I never believed in that. I was only looking out for our small farm and that seemed real from the news of the bombing in the South. My mother and father and my younger brothers and sisters needed protection and I was going to give it to them. But who knew that it would be years? I've grown old fighting this war and even though the end has to be near, I'm almost an old man. I haven't been able to marry for I was too young upon leaving for the front and now maybe I'm too old. If it hadn't been for my relationship with Hoa, I would not ever have even come close to knowing woman. Now that's all I want, all that I dream of."

He comes back to reality as he sees three helicopters letting down for a landing close to where the bombs have exploded. He stands watching for some time…until the aircraft eventually leave the valley. He turns and begins walking into the thicker vegetation, back where he knows he'd find his unit. They'll be missing him. His scouting mission should not have taken this long. As he strolls along the trail his mind wanders once again to the girl Hoa. She lived on the fringe of Thai Nguyen not far from his village. He liked that. She was more sophisticated than the girls he knew from his neighborhood. And she was beautiful. She had filled his dreams for years, and now, he had no assurances that he would ever see her again.

Chanh follows a trail through the jungle, arriving at a small encampment where he is greeted and questioned by Captain Bao.

"I see you finally decided to join up with your unit Sgt. Chanh. Where the hell have you been?"

"Sorry Chief. I fell asleep in the sun on one of the hill tops then watched the American's bombing down below. I don't know who their targets were."

"Well, I do know. It was Sgt. Lap's platoon and they lost two men. Weren't even able to extract their bodies. No matter for you because they went out early this morning on a scouting trip and ran into a small patrol of secret American troops who were wiped out by their own bombers. Our soldiers that were shot by them were just down from the North. It was their first time out. Well, at least they didn't have to spend years here like you and me. Maybe for the best."

"Maybe not Chief. Two more young men with no life. And what for? If you spend too many years on this 'great patriotic' journey you really wonder if it's all worth it."

"Keep it up Sergeant Chanh and you will require political counseling. For now, get back to your men and run a patrol around the perimeter. No telling who might be in this vicinity after that operation."

Chanh enters the interior of the campsite and gathers his men who had been lounging around enjoying their time off. This morning they had been the lucky ones. They disappeared into jungle that was heavily forested in this section which left it unviewable from the air. The Americas had sprayed much of this valley years earlier but had missed this fringe and up into the peaks a short distance to the north. The staging area for the NVA in that direction, Base 611 had still not been detected by the Puppet Troops, or their American friends.

That evening the men were sitting at primitive benches having a late meal. They had come across a small deer on patrol, so happiness pervades the compound. These soldiers carried their rice with them but had to scrouge up anything else more often than not. Wild vegetables and meat were needed to sustain them at some level of fighting condition and tonight they were a happy group of soldiers. Two of the younger troops were talking quietly about the village girls that they had known back home.

"I loved that little girl Vieng" said Private Cuong. "You remember her Huu. I know you do because you were after her too."

"Yes my good friend Cuong, I was after her… and unlike you I caught her one day out in the paddy when we were herding the ducks. Oh, so sweet she was."

"You lie Huu. She would never go with you. She loves me" said Cuong.

"Yes, I know my old friend, but she shared her sweetness with me."

At that a fight erupts and upsets the decorum of the evening. The Chief took them to task.

"Stick with the mission you two. The time will come when there will be no fight left in you" he said, "no fight at all."

Sgt. Chanh took over and settled the two men, boys really and they went back to cleaning up what was left of the evening meal, lying back with their last cup of tea.

Chanh finally was able to lie back in his hammock which he had strung between two trees on the edge of the campsite. He liked sleeping outside, away from the men that he had spent so many years fighting alongside…the few that were left from the beginning. Many of the younger replacements did not yet have a grasp on the reality of this long and nasty war. He closed his eyes, resting and his mind once again drifted back to his younger years in Tam Lap.

He had known Hoa for years when they were children playing and working in the fields along with their families and the water buffalos and the ever-present ducks that somehow always lived well on the fringe of the fields and streams. It was only a short time before they were mobilized into the army that he thought of her as a love interest, and he even then was wondering why. Hoa was an evanescence girl who spread her gaiety among whoever was in her presence. She was exhibiting a budding, womanly beauty that more boys than Chanh were becoming aware of. He began to stick closer to her whenever possible…and she seemed to like him.

He was remembering a time not so long before he had left for the front when he had been with her along the edge of a cornfield that bordered the nut trees and a fruit orchard that the village farmed communally. They were snuggling together a few rows in from the trees, and he was even almost stroking her breasts. In reality, each was too shy to go beyond sniffing each other's cheek. But they did talk of what might become of them after he returned from the war for it seemed to be a forgone conclusion that he would soon be on the trail South. It also began to look like they would have a long term future together, even though more intimacy would be necessary between them before thoughts of permanency could be a topic of conversation. The two of them lay close together under the afternoon sun each dreaming of a future as one.

Chanh was thinking of the opportunity he had missed with her as he lay in his hammock. He had always imagined how it would be to make love hidden in the corn field with a pretty village girl. And Hoa was not just a pretty girl, she was 'the' girl. The memory of his desire for her from those early years had stayed with him. He'd have to get back to see her somehow soon. He smiled at himself with thoughts of her, the prettiest girl he'd ever known, as he drifted off to sleep.

Because of the red, fertile soil in Chanh's small part of Vietnam, Tam Lap had been spared much of the hardship that people in the cities and towns and even in the large rice growing regions of the red river delta had suffered. Since so much of the rice and other crops that were grown in this most productive region in Northern Vietnam were needed to supply the troops and workers along the trail south, as well as the standing army that was fighting there. Not so much was left for the people that grew it.

The government controlled the distribution of all foodstuffs, but especially rice which was needed to keep Hanoi and the larger towns fed. That again limited what could be left to feed the farmers and their families who grew it. After some years of depreciation many were souring on the war, 'the great war' for the liberation of the South.

Suddenly there was a huge commotion in the camp. It was pitch dark and even though guards were posted on the perimeter somehow something had happened. There was a loud roar.

Chanh was up out of the hammock and immediately on his feet. "It has to be a tiger. You men be still. I'll find a light."

He dug in his gear for a small flashlight and shined it in the direction of the roar. At about the same time someone lights a lamp. The tiger was pawing through the cache of food. Cuong was up also with his AK, but was afraid to fire because of superstition, perhaps thinking it might be a ghost. Before Chanh or the other men who were now awake were able to use their weapons, the tiger left as quickly as he had arrived.

"Cuong" said Chanh, "how the hell are you going to shoot the puppet troops or the Americans if you're afraid of a tiger?"

"I'm afraid of a tiger Sargent. They are of the spirit world. I am not afraid of the puppet troops or the Americans. I even shot one when coming down the trail to my posting here in the A Shau."

"Really, why did I never hear of that?"

"Because you never asked me" said Cuong. "I am not one to brag."

"Well tell us what happened" said Chanh, "No more sleep for us. The sun will be up soon."

Corporal Cuong was a talker, and he dove into his story with relish.

"We were still in Laos. Maybe fifty K north of Base 611 where there is a good road beneath the jungle canopy. I was in the back of a truck going along in the early morning. There was not such good visibility along the road due to the thick jungle. It had grown back from the American spray and the ground cover was much thicker than it normally is. However, I have good eyes. I saw a flash on the edge of the road. A very quick flash but one long enough for me get a fix on the spot it came from. I was in the back of the truck leaning against the tailgate and just happened by luck to see it."

"Well did you shoot then," said Chanh.

"No Sargent, I did not dare to for it might have been one of ours. I jumped out of the truck. We were not going very fast. The light moved and I could make out a large man. Too big for us so I though fuck it and shot. He screamed. I lay flat on the ground and the following truck stopped while men from many trucks now jumped out. They began firing and running towards the target area. There was quick return fire and one of ours went down, but I think the enemy ran fast because there were so many of us. We went into the trees and found only one dead man. He was a black man and must be American. We had never seen one before, but we had heard stories that they were the fiercest fighters of all, except for the Koreans. We could find no one else so were ordered to load up and continue our journey."

"So you were a kind of hero Cuong" said Chanh. "Right Captain Bao."

"Yes he was" said the Chief. "It must have been one of the American spy teams that are still active. Not many are left we are told, but good for you Corporal Cuong."

With that the men began their morning duties. They were hoping that there might be something more than a ball of rice for the first and sometimes the only meal of the day. The cooks had begun working before the story had ended so there was much hope. Food seemed to always be scarce with NVA troops. The distance was so great and difficult this far down the Ho Chi Minh Trail. On occasion though the local men from the Katu tribe supplied the army with meat and vegetables, which was a rare treat. Even fresh eggs were not unheard of.

CHAPTER 5:

THE BAMBOO

BARNS AND I ARE NURSING OUR BEERS AS VAN LY attempts to engage us in conversation.

"You two need to get with it" she says. "My people have to pick up the pieces every day after the bombing. I have family on the other side. They say after the B-52 comes, there are no pieces to pick up….so, you be lucky."

We're quiet for a moment. Food for thought perhaps.

"Van Ly, how about a couple of whiskey cokes? The beer isn't doing it," says Jake Barns.

"I can do that for you Major Jake, however I think it will not work. It never does for any one of you that I serve drinks to. Even the Captain. Is that not right my Captain?"

"I'm afraid Miss Van Ly that you are correct, however we must keep trying. One mustn't ever give up on burying the truth."

"You people bury the truth every day and refuse to see it. We do see, we who live here," said Van Ly. "I wonder sometime, why does not everyone in this war turn around and go home?"

Barns looks at Winslow and smiles, "You know Ed, she's right. If we all, and I mean all sides and factions, would just turn around and go home this cluster fuck of a war would be over. Very simple solution. Now about those whiskey cokes Van Ly, make them doubles if you please."

We sat in silence again….until Van Ly is able to locate another bottle of bourbon whiskey. She's having a problem.

"Ok you officers of the great American Army, a choice must be made here. Can do?"

"Always Van Ly, we always can do. What do you require?"

"Always we have Ten High whiskey for GI. I no can find. I can sell for you some Early Times or some Wild Turkey. For me I cannot say. I no drink whiskey….just water and tea."

"Open the Turkey, Van Ly" says Barns. "Ed here will choose the Early Times just to save a few cents."

"No, it be ok" she said. "Same, same I sell for you. Fifty P each kind."

I have to smile at Barns' reply. The brands never matter to me; it's the touch. If a choice has to be made considering cost, I'd order Courvoisier XO….which is worth a few cents more. With PX pricing it's all virtually free… and you knew the supplies here came from that source.

"Actually, Van Ly, do you have any Courvoisier? If so, I can do."

"Only for you Captain Ed, and I no charge more. Maybe you can tip me."

Obviously, we would tip her and actually from what I knew of Van Ly that is all any of her customers would ever be doing with her. She was very quiet regarding her romantic life and fended off any personal inquiries…. or advances.

"All I can say Van Ly is that you are lucky Banks and Omar aren't here because you'd be selling the whole bottle for the price of Ten High," offered Barns.

"If other GI be here, I charge double. For you my good friends there be special price"

We have not discussed the day's operation, Barns and I, but we have to address today's tragedy. Why were those young troops even out there? What kind of intelligence matters a damn? We know the score. The NVA are slowly taking control.... period. How many more are going to die reaffirming that fact?

"So, Jake, what's it about....the whole fucking day? I don't mind playing the game and finishing up here but 'fuck me dead' as Sandy would say.... why?"

"Come on, get with it Ed. You know why. It's what we do. Keep the Green Machine moving along. Not much else matters. We were lucky. I've gone in as a Dust Off more than once when we lost more men among the rescuers than those we were trying to pull out. Not to mention the machines. As I said, today we were lucky. No choppers down. No fighters down. If the truth be told, we haven't controlled the A Shau since the Cav pulled out after Delaware in '68. That's seven fucking years ago. However, we are going to have to deal with the real world here fairly soon."

I've had enough talk of the war and of the military. Lien had begun working back at the Bamboo again but hadn't shown so I decide to leave and go look her up...before Omar or Banks stop in and then I'll never get out of here.

And then there was Peters....Capt. Leonard Peters from the now defunct at least as far as Viet Nam goes, 1st MI Battalion from the Saigon of the old days. He'd pulled one like me. Re-enlisted after leaving in the late Sixties apparently so he could be a witness to the end. There had been a slot open for military intelligence advisor with the ARVN up here and he'd fina-gled it. I figure on checking back in here if I'm not able to find Lien.

However, I'm a lucky man. Lien is in our love nest on Tran Phu Street so that is that for the rest of the evening. But now after the love making and the brief orgasmic slumber, I'm unable to sleep. Lien has no such trouble, so I nuzzle her cheek and go for a walk back down by the river, eventually ending up at the Bamboo. Why not one more nightcap?

They're all still there. Barns, Omar, Banks, Peters and Everest who is another holdover from earlier times. He is Lt. Arthur Everest. A few years back he was on a Navy Seal team that assassinated for the Phoenix Program in the countryside surrounding Hue. Back here today he's a bit secretive about his position with the ARVN. He might also have something to do with the patrols like the one that went bad today that are usually staffed by US forces. You'd think a few locals on those teams would be a great help but that's seldom the case. At any rate Art Everest, like myself. appears to be here for the duration. Rather like Omar but with a long break in between.

Van Ly servs me a 33. She's taller than most Vietnamese with a more substantial body. She's quite something and has the brains to go with it. If I weren't with Lien, I'd surely give her a try.

"Don't look at me that way Captain Ed. I be no fool."

I smiled, a bit embarrassed and apologize for my look. You can't fake out the Vietnamese women. They know everything. That's one reason the enemy is always one jump ahead of us. Vietnamese women work at clerical jobs in most of the headquarters country wide…and they have since the fifties. We're such a brilliant country.

"I'll tell you something Ed, the Navy Lieutenant here has opened up just a bit on his knowledge of Da Nang operations. He was the officer in charge of the LURP team that we were trying to bail out today. Isn't that right Arthur?" says Barns.

"I'll fill him in some other time Major. I can't go through it again. It makes me sick."

Omar and Banks are playing pool. Len Peters is listening to our conversation at the end of the bar. He's ordinarily a bit reticent…however he dropped that for a moment.

"I know the common, misinformed US military man loves tagging military intelligence an oxymoron, and most of the time I'd agree. But there are occasions when we are in the know...like right now. That team was able to radio in information that could be extremely important very shortly. Tragic though it was, we might be a jump ahead of NVA movements in the near future. Remains to be seen, but my feeling is that it will save some lives on our side."

By now Omar and Banks had joined the bar and are listening to Peters.

"But what about our boys," said Banks. "I don't want to get off on any of this gook shit you hear so often but fuck it man, once again we wiped out our own men. So how many Vietnamese lives do you think they were worth, Capt. Peters?"

"Well for me all lives have the same value...except for my own....just joking boys. To be serious, you're right. Lives saved at this point are mostly Vietnamese. They're doing the fighting. Granted no one seems to know why. If we couldn't whip'em there's no way these guys can, but that's where we're at. That's why we're here. Play it out till the end or go home, those are the choices. And it looks like all of us here are staying...and playing it out, so let's cut the bullshit and save all the lives that we can, white, black or yellow."

No replies right off and I'm thinking I should have stayed with Lien and left these guys mulling over the same tiresome topic that none of us are able to affect. Quite frankly I'm more interested in figuring how Lien is going to leave whenever it all falls in...and it will...sooner than later. And I wasn't sure she would leave. She has an attachment to her country, and certainly to her family that lives in the North. Her main problem would be due her relationship with me and other Americans if she remains in Da Nang after if falls.

Van Ly catches my ear at the end of the bar, so I ordered one last Courvoisier and listened.

"What do you think Capt. Ed? I am in between girl. My family is revolutionary, but I work for the Americans. Where can I go?"

"Back home and lie low" I say.

"You don't understand my Captain. I am from Hue and I do come from a revolutionary family but everyone know that I live in Da Nang and work with the Americans. And I send money to them but they still no like. It be a difficult life."

Van Ly begins talking of her life before Da Nang, and since the others were still mulling over the day's military operation, I decide to stay with her and listen.

"Even though we were a revolutionary family we still are with the mainstream in Hue, as is much of the city. The leaders of the revolution against the French were from here and went to school here. That was the Quoc Hoc High School which the French founded in 1896 to train administrators for their colonies. I went to school in the very building that Ho Chi Minh attended as well as Vo Nguyen Giap. They were the main men, and were the leaders when Viet Nam defeated the French at Dien Bien Phu. It was the first time a colony defeated the hated Colonialists in the whole world. We were a proud people in Hue and I was slated to begin school in the University, but trouble kept happening."

"Yes, I recall" I mention. "First there was the Buddhist insurrection in '63. Protesters burned down the American Cultural center in 1965, but that was before your time Van Ly. You're still a young girl."

"Thank you, my Captain, but I am not so young…just look young. All Vietnamese women look young…then they look old. No in between."

"Well" I told her, "you are certainly on the young side of 'in between' and all of us here are aware of it." She smiles at that and continues.

"Even with all that trouble it looked like I could be a student at the University in 1968 but then Tet happened. After that I no be nothing. Just work bar for GI."

"What about it Ed, you ready to hit the sack? I am," said Barns.

I looked his way and saw that the others had left.

34

"One more Courvoisier Barns and I'm with you. For both of us Van Ly, and we will go and let you sleep. But first fill me in on how you survived the great Tet of '68."

She pours us both a good snifter of cognac and continues.

"It was very difficult. We have to watch both sides. The NVA and VC who came into town do not know everybody so there is some risk. My family should be alright but who can know what the outsiders will think? And who can know who the Americans will kill? So, you see it was very difficult for my family."

"If I remember correctly" says Barns, "Hue was free of US military for the most part, at least before Tet. The action I was familiar with was in Phu Bai that was a few miles south at the airport. And of course, the 1st Cav. base camp at Evans ten or twelve klicks on Rt. One North, then a few more inland, if memory serves me correctly."

Van Ly pours herself a cognac… and she doesn't drink. "I can say that our people were bad enough, but there were too many Americans. Bombing, shooting everywhere. Blowing up the houses. helicopters, airplanes dropping fire. It seemed to go on forever. But it did end, the violence that is. The pain and the misery continued for a long time. I left and came down here. No need for more. I like to forget."

We stay quiet sipping our cognac. Then Barns pipes in. "What about now in Hue, Van Ly? When does it end?"

"Wait and see is what I can say. Who can know?"

With that we finally leave. I touch her hand as I walk by. She looks lost in sadness.

Next morning I joined them in the mess for breakfast. Barns, Peters and Everest were having a black coffee officers conference, so I fill a mug and sit at the end of the table, remaining quiet while they continue their conversation. A funny thing here, I'm familiar with Art Everest from my youth back in Northern New York. His mother had been great friends with my aunt who lived a few miles north of Port Kent on Lake Champlain. We had met a few times back then, on those long summers when we were young, at family picnics at their camp on the west side of Cumberland Head. But I hadn't seen him since those days until a recent chance meeting when I was in Saigon staying at the Rex BOQ. We spent a long evening drinking and talking at that BOQ's rooftop bar. It was just corner ways across the square from the Caravelle, the most famous rooftop in Saigon. We closed out the evening there, among the crowd of newsmen that were still left in town covering the war.

It turned out he'd been 'in country' with Seal teams a number of times. On thinking back, I had remembered that he'd gone in the service a few months before myself back in the mid-sixties. But he was still active and operating in Vietnam during these last days as some sort of undercover operations type. He never made that clear to me and still hasn't after some days up here in Da Nang.

"So what's up boys? Anything happening today that I'm unaware of?"

"Well, I'll tell you what Winslow, we thought you were the boss." said Barns

"Never happen GI. Aren't I the lowest ranking man here?"

"No time for this, men. I'm off to headquarters. I'm not the lowest ranking man here and I do have something to do," said Everest.

With that he left, and Peters followed. Barns and I looked at each other for a minuet…and started laughing.

"It's hard for me to take anything serious at the moment" I say, "and they'll be learning the same soon enough."

After leaving Barns, I check in with Gen. Le Quang Luang the CO of the ARVN Airborne Division that I'm attached to. He indicates a slow day, so I'm on my own.

A slow day… but a beautiful, cool morning with a bright sun…so I walk from the airfield down through town past Lien's place on Tran Phu, down to Bach Dang along the river and finally stop in to see Emerson Fitz. He manages the IVS office that supports war refugees in Da Nang, as well as the surrounding area.

International Voluntary Services was one of the few, effective relief organizations operating in the war arena and Emerson had been at the helm here a number of years before I arrived. He was sitting out front having a coffee enjoying the heat from the morning sun. I pull up a stool beside him and sit down. He looks up.

"Winslow…what the hell man, I thought you'd have left by now."

'Never happen Fitz. I'm sticking around till we wrap it up… however that goes. Besides, I like my Lien and so far, she's staying."

Then he said, "Chi also. Says she won't leave either, but I figure when push comes to shove, she will. There's a whole world out there besides this place, not counting the present scene here. And she needs to see the world. Too confining here."

"For sure", I said. "That is for sure."

We sit there in silence for some minuets enjoying the scene along with the sun's warmth. The fleet was in the harbor and a number of the fishing boats are tied up at the pier across the street. They are the blue boats with the red eyes painted on the prow. Quite beautiful. The fish are long gone.

I'll tell you what," said Emerson. "I've got to make a run over the pass and look in on a family that has had some very bad luck. I won't be long there, but the ride takes a while and it's always pleasant. Sometimes terrifying if you consider the traffic… but always pleasant."

I decide to take him up on it. Hai Van Pass, one of the great sights in Vietnam, can be a life-threatening experience. Twelve, fifteen miles of highway full of hairpin turns, topping off at fifteen hundred feet or so. It can be a challenge considering the heavy military traffic along with the crazy trucks that pass for a civilian trucking market. They're mostly junkers with bad brakes. But this morning we'll take on the challenge.

Emerson and I cruise straight to the top of the pass in his old Renault without a hitch. We pull over by the pill box bunkers that were built by the French during their war and are presently manned by ARVN soldiers. Then it happens….a loud outburst of machine gun fire. We leap out and hit the ground behind the Renault. There is no more gunfire, so eventually, slowly we rise to our feet and look toward the bunkers. Who walks over but Everest and Omar. They notice us so saunter across…probably to see if we're in one piece.

"Not to worry boys. It's taken care of," says Everest. "Omar's on top of it, but the mole ran and disappeared into the brush before they opened up with the M 60."

'How the hell did you two get up here ahead of me ?" I ask.

"The Major and his Huey. They dropped us off and flew on to Phu Bai. Peterson had been looking into what he suspected was a spy for the VC that was leaking information on troop movements along the top of the pass here Omar spent some time digging for info with the shift on duty and when he was getting close, the suspected culprit leaped out the back and disappeared. They opened up a little too late. You always wonder if there was more complicity than what seems obvious, but what can you do? It's no good for anyone to be on the losing side."

Emerson offers them a ride back when he's finished his work, but they're in no hurry.

"Have to talk to the girls here and see what they know" says Omar with a smile on his face. "Maybe they be VC, who can know?"

"You two go ahead," says Everest, "but thanks anyway. I'll poke around her for a spell and see what comes up."

He has a point. A cool morning up in the fresh air with a view to kill. Young girls flirting around, selling cokes and whatever. Who could ask for more in the middle of a bad war?

Emerson has been quiet. As we drive down the back side he opens up.

"If I get killed here it'll be you fuckers, not the VC. I've driven over this pass a hundred times and never a shot. Once with you, Winslow, and all hell breaks loose, and not just here. You'll see when we arrive at our destination."

He's right about that. We pull in at a small house as the landscape levels off on the Hue side of the pass. This is not an upscale neighborhood to say the least. However Emerson knows his way around and the couple who live here invite us inside. He speaks great Vietnamese, better than myself, so I miss some of the conversation. Eventually we walk to the rear of the house, that overlooks rice paddy land and is fairly well lit. A young girl is lying on a cot. She is horribly scarred on one side of her face and down her shoulder along one arm. The skin is drying up. It looks as if this has happened some time ago, but is slow in healing.

"It's worse than this if you take off her clothes," said Emerson "Why describe it? You know what I mean."

"Was this caused by what I'm thinking," I ask

"Right. It sure as fucking hell was. Napalm. What kind of scum would do this to a beautiful young girl? You know Winslow, if someone poured gasoline on her and touched it off, he'd be strung up or beaten to death. If one of your fucking compadres is the culprit from the air, he gets a medal. You ever think about that?"

I can't answer him. I'm raining tears. I bid the parents farewell and leave for the car. In due course he joins me, and we drive back towards the top of the pass in silence. No action around the pill box bunkers at the top, so we push on down the other side towards Da Nang.

"Emerson, I don't bomb people. I don't drop napalm on them."

"You're part of the machine, man… you help." And then, "Sorry about that Ed. It got to me. I've been trying to help them with her, but you can see it's almost hopeless."

"I know what you mean about men who kill from the air. Somehow they don't see it….or don't choose to see it."

For some time we drive along in silence. Dusk settles in as we pull up in front of his office.

"Ok Winslow, my heads clear. Let me drag this crate around back, then we can stop in for a beer."

We walk down the street to the Bamboo saying little. Back here things are pleasant enough. Most of the fishing fleet is still tied to the pier, so if one doesn't look afar, the military presence here appears limited. As we walk into the bar, I can see Lien talking with Van Ly. She must have begun her shift early. In fact, this is where we met, but her present job as an interpreter in the offices of the Airborne Division limits her time. Actually, this rather ramshackle establishment is the unofficial headquarters for a certain type of US military living in Da Nang. Most of the people I work with are part of it. Enlisted and Officers. And of course Omar, the ultimate survivor.

I walk over to Lien and squeeze her hand. She does not like expressions of intimacy in public. And neither do most of the girls who work in these places, that at one time proliferated everywhere the American GI lived and worked. Under considerably trying circumstances they did their best to maintain a modicum of decency. Most of them would never have been anywhere near bars, much less 'short time' houses. They were the lifeline for their families. There was no economy and they had nothing else to sell. The pretty daughter or sister or even the mother at times, was sacrificed for the family's survival.

"Where you go my captain. I look all day," asks Lien. "I think maybe you run away from Lien."

I smile and sniff her cheek.

"That will never happen Lien. I am with you forever….as I have spoken to you so many times."

I hate coming across as a lovesick teenager, but what can I do? Emerson is quietly sitting by himself down the bar, and it's not such a large one. I slide down to try and perk him up.

"What's Chi up to," I ask.

"Like I want to see her right now. That girl we looked in on is one of her many cousins. And what could I do to help. Just about nothing....fucking nothing."

"Don't keep punishing yourself Emerson, for Christ's sake. You're not a surgeon."

"I have to admit, when the US was here in force, I was able to acquire most anything I needed in the way of supplies or services when an emergency like this occurred. Not with the ARVN who run the war now. They want money for anything. I've heard of troops in the field under fire from the NVA that have had to pay for artillery support... by the shell. There's no fucking way they can win this thing."

" I hate to blame them for all of it. General Luong tells me that they've had to pay people at the port to keep the supply chain going. It's tough for them too."

"I suppose you're right," he comes back with. "They're all just trying to survive....rather like us. However, to not drop the subject entirely, you guys are still running most of the air support and that's what's doing the damage that I'm supposed to be fixing."

"Oh man, let's talk about something else. I'm tired. Van Ly... two Courvoisier please."

Van Ly servs them up and then drops in her own two cents. "Why don't you two go home to your girlfriends and forget about war talk. It's all I hear from you both lately."

"For sure" says Lien who had been listening in but saying little. "I love to go home with my Captain."

"After we finish this drink my sweet one...only be a few minutes." I want to get right with Emerson first.

"Well in another context, Emerson, what about Chi?. I know I haven't stopped by your office lately."

"Oh, she's good....we're good. Even if this war doesn't end soon, she and I have to leave for a time. It's too much. The problem is, like most of them... their families; And I certainly understand but hell sometimes you've gotta just take a chance and let things fall where they may."

"That not be so easy," says Lien. "If we leave for a small trip and the war end wrong, what can we do. Our family be here forever. Maybe ok... but maybe not."

This kind of conversation continues till finally we do leave to spend the night with our girlfriends. Since Lien and I are just one street down from his office, Emerson and I decide to meet for coffee early on the street in front where a one-legged guy sets up every morning to earn his daily bread. I presume he lost the leg in some operation here but since he's never brought it up neither have I.

Dawn is breaking as I walk back to catch Emerson for that early morning coffee. A jeep cruises by with Barns, and Banks who's driving. They pull over to talk. Emerson still hasn't arrived and if he does while they're here, I hope his mind has moved on from the girl who'd been napalmed. Let's face it, Barns flew choppers who at the very least had door gunners....often times trigger happy door gunners, which never bodes well for Vietnamese farmers and their families.

It turns out that they're on a mission looking for a part needed to keep the Huey in the air. They're driving to a supply depot at the Navy deep water port across the river just west of Monkey Mountain. Emerson shows up shortly after they moved on and he's upbeat, like usual which is a requirement for a job like his.

We're sitting quietly sipping that black sweet coffee the Vietnamese are so adept at making, watching the fisherman prepping their boats to head back out to sea when Van Ly walks by. She smiles at us and hesitates for a moment.

"Hey, Van Ly.... Grab a stool and let me buy you a coffee."

"Yes, I can do that this morning Capt. Winslow," she answers, "I go for early walk to wake up from late night. When you leave other GI come and stay very late. I no like. They work with Lt. Everest and are very loud, very tough."

"Well, it's a new day Van Ly, so let's start fresh. Forget about yesterday and tough guy Lt. Everest…and his men."

That works and we settle down for a second coffee with Van Ly. She begins talking with Emerson about some issue with a local family. It seems strange to me that this beautiful girl never appears to be involved with any man… local or American. There's a rule, possibly unwritten, for a girl working a bar here. Despite what most of these yahoos think, these girls are not an easy mark. The rule is to never sleep with a customer…never. They will keep coming back trying and buying drinks forever, but let it happen just once and things change. Now they think she's 'just a whore' like all the rest…and they tell all their friends. So they all move on to another bar, and fantasize about the newest girl they hope to conquer.

Take Lien for instance. When I met her she was working at the Bamboo. I was older and not in the market for a short time girl. For me it was time for a mate and after getting to know her, it still nearly took a marriage proposal before we became intimate. At any rate Van Ly needs someone like me…. or so I think. Though more than likely she has a life unknown to all of us. I've seen movies and read plenty of books on the resistance movements in Europe during WW II and imagine they are at least as adept here. But I've seen nothing indicating that in my circle.

"So Van Ly, what have you got going on today?" She looks at me and says, "maybe I need another coffee."

The one legged guy hears and goes to work on her order. Someday I have to get his story, or just ask Emerson. He must know. At any rate Van Ly is served her coffee but remains silent.

Then, "Maybe nothing Capt. Winslow, maybe nothing." And that was it, so I left it that way.

"Well, it is a beautiful morning at least." And she agrees with that.

" I do have something to do today," says Emerson suddenly. "I support a clinic down in Ky La, just west of Marble Mountain and it was shot up recently by some asshole in a Huey. Let's hope it wasn't Banks, the crew chief and gunner that makes up Barns' crew. Of course, if it was them, they'd probably have a medal by now."

"Please Emerson, can't we drop that?"

"I'll drop it when it stops."

"Well, what happened? What are you going to do there?"

"Initially just express some concern. No aid from the government so far. Neither ARVN nor MACV. No correct that… DAO… Defense Attaché Office I think they call it now. Makes no difference in the end. Same frame of mind. Bomb the gooks."

"Please Emerson. We know. Spare us more." I pleaded with him.

"Don't get me wrong Winslow. Like I was saying yesterday I've had quite good support from the US military, whether it was MACV, USARV or now the DAO. At times they all have been generous with various supplies, be it building materials, food or medicine. If they'd just stop killing these people, the fucking idiots. OK… I'm done. Gotta get a moving on."

He jumps up, kicked over his Honda and hits the road. Van Ly watches him go and smiles.

"I like your friend Emerson. He good man. I know about the trouble in Ky La. My uncle lives there, and he saw. Helicopter fly low over rice paddy. Man and his son who work in fields see, then run towards clinic. They shoot them when they get to door. Man killed and son hurt and bullets go into the building. Hurt nurse and woman who having baby. No good. Very bad in this village who have trouble many years with soldier. With VC, as well as American and ARVN. Americans kill more people. They suspect some village people maybe help VC. My uncle say that the village want no more war. They don't care who wins."

"That is not good certainly Van Ly, but Major Barns has never told me of anything like this for a long time. I don't think he is the man. I hope not."

I need to move this conversation forward. Actually, I have to head over to Marine Headquarters and check in with General Luong. I've a feeling that things are not what they seem with the unit that I spend so much time with. A bad feeling.

CHAPTER 6:

_____

NVA BASE 611

BASE 611 IS THE STAGING AREA FOR THE NVA. IT'S LOCATED at the north end of the A Shau Valley which is twenty-seven miles long. The Rao Lao River runs its full length. This valley is surrounded by the Trung Son Mountains which rise up to three thousand meters. Much of it is covered with elephant grass that towers above a normal man's head, in spite of the fact that this area was sprayed with Agent Orange many times. The heavy rainfall in this part of the country explains the great growth of vegetation as well of the fact that regrowth after spraying is thicker than the original ground cover. And there are tigers in these mountains, large ones. The only permanent population in this sector are members of the Katu tribe which are suspected supporters of the NVA. If the Americans had been able to maintain control of this area for any length of time, perhaps they would have supported them.

Base 611 is nearly invisible from the air for much of it was dug in underground among the higher trees in the valley close to the border with Laos. Two men in the uniform of the People's Army of Viet Nam are sitting on a primitive wooden bench alongside an equally primitive table having tea and talking quietly.

It's Sargent Chanh with his superior officer Captain Bao.

"The thing is Chief, if I am not able to take a short leave now, I might never make it back home. With any luck I could catch rides on empty tucks back up the trail towards Hanoi and pick up some local transport home to Thai Nguyen. Just two or three days in my home would be enough."

"If you are given permission Sgt. Chanh, who will perform your duties while you are absent?"

"Corporal Chung can handle things Chief. He knows the operation. Things are pretty quiet presently, but they may not be much longer. Now or never for me."

The Chief sips his tea and responds slowly. "I will approve your pass Sgt. Chanh. You will proceed to Thai Nguyen using military transport and report back here as soon as you can. Good luck. You can pack your things and leave immediately."

Sgt. Chanh rises and bows towards his commanding officer, shakes his hand then ducks down into a bunker to let Chung know that he is in charge. The bunker has a roof that is layered with earth a couple of feet thick. Daylight and air are able to enter beneath this covering since the roof is raised on stilt like supports. Chanh is able to go over the limited plans for the next couple of weeks. The unit has been in somewhat of a holding pattern since their latest engagement with US Airpower and intends to lay low until plans come down from higher headquarters for an engagement that might have lasting effect on the opposition.

The two soldiers, the bo doi from the north, bid each other fare well as Chanh throws his small pack over his shoulder and heads out up the trail from Base 611 north towards Mu Gia Pass where the Trail enters Laos. After years of living under incessant bombing from the Americans, the Vietnamese had still been able to construct a hard road for the length of the Trail up into North Vietnam to connect with their roadways. Over the course of the trail's existence well over forty thousand peasants from Vietnam and Laos were pressed into service to maintain and enlarge it to where it is now, as Chanh begins his homeward trek. These laborers were both men and women, mostly young. Within half a day Chanh meets up with two girls who are walking along a portion not so far from the A Shau, that is still dirt though there is an oil pipeline along this section. They are charged with overseeing any damage that might require repairs to keep the whole operation going.

"Hello there" says Chanh as he approaches the girls who look up.

"Hello to you" they both responded. Then one, the younger prettier one, says "and where are you going bo doi?"

"I'm on my way home to Thai Nguyen and hope to pick up a ride on a truck going in that direction. I am Chanh."

"We have no names" she says smiling. "We are called beautiful girls."

That's how a friendly conversation begins between Chanh and the girls. They invite him to sit in the shade along the road and take a long drink of water from their canteen. He is glad to oblige. After a brief rest, considering they work this area, he asks them about the possibility of catching a ride on a truck. They inform him that during the day there is very little truck traffic for the obvious reason that they all lived under the constant possibility of American Bombing.

"I passed through walking down this trail many years ago." he explains to them.

During those early years there was no roadway, only a network of footpaths that were serviced by bicycles carrying freight throughout the journey south. A pole was fixed to the handlebars which allowed a porter to steady and steer his two wheeled transport that could carry on occasion up to a thousand pounds of freight. The replacement soldiers, the bo doi, walked the whole distance carrying their pack, rifle, ammunition and rice.

"It looks much easier today" Chanh tells the girls. He is in no mood to flirt. They seemed to be, but at this time, even considering the lack of female companionship over the last many years, he is headlong pushing forward towards his goal. Home, and a visit with Hoa, the girl who might be the one who could erase the memory of this crazy and difficult war.

"Well, goodbye girls. I must move on. They didn't give me much time away from my unit."

"Wait for us," the younger girl says. "I will tell you how to do this and make your trip faster."

They walk along together for a while, and she explains the method used to traverse the Truong Son Supply Route.

'It really should be easy for you. Only two kilometers ahead there is a relay base where the road clears off for the day and trucks are reloaded for the next leg of the journey. They will head back up the Trail to the next stop by morning and then reload for the return. You must just keep catching the return truck. Soon you be in Hanoi."

Both girls laughed heartedly at that remark. Chanh thanks them profusely and walks on towards the relay station. Just before reaching that destination, he hears a helicopter approaching and jumps in the ditch among the brush. He has to be careful when traversing this route during the daytime.

The undergrowth along this portion of the Trail is not that heavy. The original jungle cover had been poisoned years ago by the Americans and their sprays. The second growth had risen beyond the brush stage but still does not cover completely the view from the air. There are places where the tops of trees on either side are tied together to provide some sort of protective canopy. Chanh is tired and thirsty once again by the time he reaches the relay station just before dusk. There are a surprising number of trucks and freight bicycles tucked among the trees along the trail where they are protected from air surveillance which comes in the form of US Fighter Bombers every morning when the skies are clear.

"Who could I see about catching a ride north," he asks the first man he sees.

"Who are you…where you going?" he asks.

Chanh explains his situation and is sent to the area headquarters of the 559th Group that's in charge of the Trung Son Highway. There's a Sargent Hai running things. He let it be known that he's too busy to bother with one man's effort to get home.

"I haven't been back to see my wife and kids for five years" he comes back with. "What's your problem?"

Chanh explains once again his position. "We all have the same problem but since I do have a chance to make it back, and have a narrow window to complete my voyage, I'm just asking for some help to continue on my way. I hope to cause no one any extra work."

The transportation Sergeant softens up. "I'm sorry. Just too busy. When the trucks head north after dark ask any of the drivers for a ride. Most love the company so they can have someone new to talk too. It's boring as hell driving up and down this road, I can tell you. There is no glory in it for us. We come under fire from fighters and B-52s and those fucking helicopters almost every day and who cares? They bury us along the road and the trucks move on. I want to go home too, for good. Fuck this whole operation….but don't mention this to anyone else. Just venting. And good luck on your trip north."

Chanh smiles at the man and pats his shoulder. "Thank you, Sergeant Hai, and good luck to you also."

The way station is beginning to be extremely busy. Trucks are being unloaded and reloaded and checked for security before heading out. Most of the ones going north are empty. They will go through the same motion after reaching the relay ahead of them. There are entertainers who work through the length of these mountains to keep morale up among the workers and security troops who work permanently at these stations. Chanh is extremely lucky for the first truck he approaches has a contingent of women on board, girls really. None of them look twenty. They all smile at him as he walks to the front of the truck.

"Is there room for me?" he asks the driver.

"For sure there is my fellow bo dai. Where you going?"

"North… to Thai Nguyen. I live near there in the village of Tan Lap."

"You go a long, long way but I can take you to the next way station and am sure you can pick up with another truck there."

"Thank you very much. My name is Chanh. What be yours?"

"Bay is me. Your driver Bay is at your command."

Chanh jumps up front. Darkness has fallen, so the trucks are lining up to leave. They most always travel by convoy in either direction for protection from the ever present attacks from the air. The two bo doi chat away for a while before Chanh, exhausted from his day long walk, falls asleep.

"Hey Sergeant, wake up. It almost getting light. You can look out for me, so I don't fall asleep before reaching the Base Area ahead. It's very big. You will like. Maybe you can talk with the girls when we stop and find some food. They are very nice girls, who I am sure would like your company".

After a short while the two bo doi with their truckload of performers arrived at the base station. The driver goes off to deal with his next load. Chanh and the girls find a mess hall where they join the line for breakfast. This eating establishment was actually a shack dug into the ground under the trees, but is quite operational. One girl in particular named Ca, is outgoing and talkative, and she's informing Chanh of the troupe's history. It turns out that at one time there were three times as many performers as are presently here, but many had been killed by air strikes and bombing over the few years since they joined the 559 Group as entertainers. It's an all-women troupe since no men can be spared from the field. National policy dictates that everyone do their duty to defeat the enemy. Potential soldiers will not be involved with any song and dance operation.

"Where do you live in the North?" Chanh asks the girl.

"My family now lives in Hanoi" answers Ca. "A long time ago they were from a village near Hai Phung but now my family and all my cousins live in Hanoi. I learned to sing and dance at the schools there. Otherwise, I would probably belong to one of the work gangs that keep this route to the South open."

"What is your name?" she inquires of him. "Where do you come from?"

"I am Chanh and am from north of Hanoi, not so far from where your family lives. It's outside of the large town of Thai Nguyen, in the village of Tan Lap. It is in the farming country, very peaceful, very beautiful. I hope to move back there when this all ends and never leave. Too many years lost."

"Keep that to yourself my friend" she says smiling. "The political commissars will hear you and it will not go well."

"My new friend Ca, of course you speak the truth, but I have been on the front lines so long I no longer care what they do or care or think. I just 'wanna go home'.

They look up as their driver approaches.

"Luck is with you…and with me. I have been ordered to continue north with your troupe Ca, to the next way station. If you'd like to ride along Chanh, you are welcome."

There were smiles all around It's time to find a place to sleep. The girls have designated quarters.

"Come with me Chanh" says Bay. "We can sleep in the truck and will be ready first thing this evening for the drive north."

Chanh wakes up early, sometime before darkness sets in, when they can be on their way. Since not much is happening, he decides to walk around the way station and do some exploring. He's absolutely astonished. As a young bo doi he walked down through this area eight years ago when it was mostly foot paths and small dirt tracks in places where it was possible for a truck to pass. He had passed over a finished two-lane road on the trip up from Base 611, something that would have been unimaginable when he had traveled through this same area on foot those many years ago.

A soldier approaches him and inquires as to his presence.

"Just looking around. It's good to see how much progress has been made since I was here last."

The soldier is some younger than Chanh, and from appearances it's clear that he hasn't been to the front. He's curious about Chanh.

"Where have you been sergeant? I haven't actually been off the trail. I spend most of my time at these way stations keeping things going. You can see that we have many trucks pulled in here under the trees. If you look closely, you will see a number of mess halls, some storage facilities that are dug in, mostly underground, and one quite well equipped repair shop."

"Yes, I can see that this is quite an operation. I've been mostly in the jungles west of Hue and Da Nang since arriving at Base 611. It's a large area and there has been some intense fighting and bombing over the years I've been there. I know they bomb the hell out of this trail, but we've come against some strong armies that the Americans have fielded in that same area. In the A Shau Valley in particular."

"I've heard of that place Sergeant and hope to be assigned to a unit there some time soon. I don't want to miss out on some real fighting before we win this thing."

"Count your blessings my boy and consider yourself lucky. So far, you've survived. No sense pushing your luck. I've buried too many young men like yourself to wish it on anyone. I think I'll move on and find one of your mess halls for some evening tea. Good luck to you."

"You too Sergeant. Stay safe."

Chanh did want some tea and hopefully an evening breakfast. Rather than look up a mess hall right off he returned to the truck to see if Bay was up and perhaps find the girls for a social meal before hitting the road.

He's lucky. Bay is awake and ready to go. He thinks he knows where the girls will be, so they wandered through a sea of trucks that preparing for the night's work till finding them at a distant, quieter mess. They joined the line, picked up their bowl of pho and grabbed a seat at the girl's table. A very primitive table situated in the mess that was half underground with an earthen roof.

Bay speaks first. "You girls load up when we're finished eating. Good morning, Ca. I hope you had a good day's rest."

In normal times perhaps these girls would be swamped with male attention. And they are to some extent. However female companionship along the trail isn't so difficult to arrange. The supply of entertainers was limited but among the huge numbers that are required to keep the trail repaired and open, are thousands of girls. Their presence among regular military units is limited, but more than made up for among the work gangs and drivers.

"Yes Bay, I enjoyed a great night's rest" answered Ca. "I think all of us girls did, and we are now ready to hit the road. We have a short performance scheduled for the drivers before they pull out for the next night's work when we arrive at the way station up ahead and will be preforming yet again for the regulars after they leave. We can always sing and dance under the trees, unseen from above during the morning before everyone heads out for sleeping."

So, it's settled. In short order Bay's truck joined up with the morning convoy heading north. It was less structured than the convoy of laden trucks heading south with their loads of ammunition and related supplies of warfare. Bay, the driver, has arranged for Ca to sit up front with him. And why not? She is a beautiful and gregarious girl, and he is in need of just that. For the company if nothing else.

"You ride in the back Chanh, I have one girl and you have many. We both be happy."

As they pulled out on the trail, Chanh is thinking that he's much more than happy, and more than lucky so far on his long trek north. Good ride and great company. The boys back in the unit wouldn't believe it. A few more days and he'd be back in Tam Lap.

But for now, he would enjoy the company of these enthusiastic and lovely young women. He begins a conversation with Hue, another more talkative one.

"What do you do Hue, during performances? Sing, dance, play an instrument, or just look beautiful."

"I just look beautiful" she replied gigging. "I am beautiful, but I can sing and dance and also play the Dan Nhi and the Sau Truc. I very talented girl." The usual banter and flirting between men and girls continues until the truck pulls over to help a stopped vehicle that was carrying wounded soldiers.

Many trucks heading north are filled with wounded from battles in the south. And they were the lucky ones. Transport from areas of battle were most often on foot. There are no helicopters or land transport to move the wounded to vehicles on the trail or the journey north. Triage is primitive to say the least. Often out in the open air, they patch up the wounded, so they'll survive the journey to the aid stations along the trail. Hospitals in the Base areas are limited, and ill equipped, but are able to facilitate a surprising number of wounded for the journey to better equipped hospitals in the Hanoi area.

Bay and Chanh immediately jump out to offer help. Luckily, it's a front wheel flat tire. The two men and the driver are able to jack up the rear and pull off the outside dual to replace the flat. In fifteen minutes, they're on their way. Chanh joins Bay up front as they pull out and rejoin the convoy.

"I've heard talk in Base 611 that there has been a large drop in B 52 bombing since Sam missiles were installed at points along the Trong Son Trail," Chanh says.

"That's true" replies Bay, "however fighters and helicopter gunships continue to pose a real problem. And you know it's not just the enemy and his bombs that slow us down. Malaria is a big problem and as you could expect we have a shortage of medicine. Then there are snakes and accidents. This is a rough road at times, especially after a bombing run by the B-52s, and some drivers are not so experienced as me. I've been driving the Trail for years. Lucky so far. And don't forget crossing bridges. There are hundreds of them…and they are under water so not to be seen from the air. They are also the only place on the roadway that is not hidden by vegetation. Very dangerous. Many drivers, soldiers and laborers have drowned over the years at these river crossings.

"What you say Bay makes me think none of us are safe. Somehow this has to end…soon I hope."

"I forgot to say about the fire. The Americans can still drop napalm from the fighters. Too low for Sam missiles. Many times they set fire to the forest and more of us die. I'm with you man. Let's end this operation and go home. Find wife to make love to. That be my goal.".

The conversation turns to women full time. Both of these men were not boys. That was when they first came down the trail. But now. nearing their mid to late twenties, they view themselves as old men… due to the preceding half dozen years being spent along the Trung Son Trail or in the jungles of southern Viet Nam. They're both looking for wives and hoping for families. Maybe a little farm in the countryside outside their home villages. Is that asking for so much?

The sun is nearly breaking as the truckload of young women, the entertainers, pulled over at the next way station amid a flurry of rocket fire from a low flying helicopter. Luckily the cover was dense enough to prevent much damage. A few trucks were hit along the periphery, with most of the rockets disappearing into the jungle foliage.

"One more time we are lucky." Says Bay who appears to know just where he was heading with the truck. "The girls will perform on a small knoll that overlooks an open space where the people heading out on trucks can see and listen. I must service my vehicle now but will look you up for our last meal together"

"Don't miss us, Bay. Who knows when or where I'll be going next," said Chanh. "I'll wait here and help the girls prepare for their show if they will let me, or just watch.".

The performers unload their few possessions from the rear of the truck, It's evident that they have already changed into clothing more appropriate for a performance. More form fitting clothes with a small smidgen of color.

Clothes that would make them stand out from the common black pajama and military uniforms that prevail throughout.

It is a hurried performance for the men and women who have spent the night driving or traveling down the Trail. Ca is the singer. Hue and a few other girls play instruments, and the rest are dancers. They hold their audience in awe, momentarily transforming its drab existence to their home villages in the North. Silence… not uproarious clapping and stomping. For this is serious, almost mystical… Ca singing with the voice of an angel. Tears prevailing.

Chanh approaches the knoll as the show ends. "How about we all eat together before your later performance."

"Yes," Ca answers. "We should have plenty of time."

They are able to find room in one of the mess halls that're like the ones at the previous way station….dug in with upper open sides and covered with an earthen roof that would provide some protection from aerial bombardment. They line up for the usual meal of pho and tea. After all, this meal has kept the Vietnamese alive for centuries.

"I loved your show," Chanh mentions, as they sit around drinking tea after finishing the meal. "We've had nothing resembling that performance in the years I've been fighting in the South. It made me cry."

"Don't cry for us," laughs Ca. "If we do not survive until final victory, we can die with the knowledge that we have done our duty. It is enough."

"I applaud you" says Chanh, "all of you, however I hope to make it till the end. Whatever my duty was, I've done it. I must move on with my life as I am sure you all will."

"Well, we are of like mind" said Ca, seriously. "Maybe I just joke a little. We all want to make it to the end of this war so we can begin a normal life too. Good luck to us all."

They all smile and agree. Then Bay shows up.

"I must grab a bite very fast for I am to drive one more leg north before picking up a load to return down the trail. You should come with me Chanh since that is the direction you are heading. You can help drive so I can get some rest. I'm heading right out because we have some wounded that need to arrive at the next way station very soon. There is a better equipped field hospital there that will help keep them alive. Two trucks going."

"I'm ready right now, Bay." Chanh replies. "All the better for me. I don't have much time to make it home and then return for what we all hope is the final offensive."

"Oh, we just meet," says Hue smiling. "We so enjoy your company. You leave too soon."

"Thank you Hue, and all you girls. Good that we enjoyed each together, but for me I must get going. Good by now and good luck all of you."

The truck, as well as another, is loaded with wounded that have to be moved forward quickly. Bay and Chanh joined the two nurses who were going to accompany them for the next leg. They load immediately, crank up the engine and head up the trail. This portion had better cover from vegetation than the previous leg. On some stretches the trees and brush has grown back faster than along other sections, after the spraying of herbicides by the Americans. Any luck and the two truckloads of wounded bo doi, would move on through in one piece. There was but one small river to cross on this leg and the water is usually low this time of year.

They've been plugging along for an hour or so when Chanh offers to take over the driving.

"Actually Bay, I'd love too. Not much of a chance where I've been living." They switch without stopping and Bay immediately falls asleep with his head against the door.

The rear of the vehicle has a canvass covering but since it's the dry season the drivers roll along with their tops down. It's possible to talk with the nurse through the opening behind the front seats. Hanh, who's tending the soldiers is leaning over the backs of the seats to talk.

"They are all resting now. I thought I'd come up front for a view and some fresh air."

"Any time" Chanh replies, "we love the company of beautiful girls."

"Oh, I am not so beautiful" she replies with a smile on her face, "just pretty."

There's an audible moan from the back, so Hanh returns to the rear of the truck to tend to her patients. Since the PAVN have no helicopters for medical evacuation and have no motorized transport into battles with the puppet troops and the Americans, the men who do make it out alive with serious wounds, are most often in bad shape. The wounded on board this truck had wounds that would prohibit them from returning to the Front but looked as if they have a good chance of surviving with the proper treatment. Others, less seriously wounded, would be able to return to their units if they survived. They're kept at better equipped field hospitals in one of the Base Areas.

Hanh leaned over the front seat once again. "My patient is ok now and sleeping so let's continue."

Chanh fills her in on his unit, the battles they've fought, great and small and his survival over the last eight or so years. He recounts his friends and fellow soldiers who will never make it home for the life they had dreamed of. He isn't even sure of how many years, it's been so long.

"Let me tell you of some of my times," Hanh says. "I've been the nurse along this stretch of highway for at least two years. Before that I spent another two years near the southern end of the Truong Son Support Route close to Loc Ninh, but in Kampuchea where we have a small field hospital and aid station. We were at the end of the line and supplies were limited, even more limited than here or anywhere along the route. Always short of medical supplies and drugs, even now but we do what we can, oftentimes with next to nothing. "

"Oh, I know what you mean," said Chanh. "Too many times I've help carry wounded off the field, carrying a stretcher for kilometers to the aid station and when we arrive there is not so much to help them. For me I am very lucky. Only minor wounds."

They continued along till signs of a river crossing became visible ahead. Chanh shakes Bay's leg to wake him up since he is familiar with the route. Bay wakens in an instant and takes over the driving.

"You've got to be careful at this crossing," said Bay. "We will be visible from the air a few minutes too long. You'll see that the bridge is a just under the surface if the water hasn't dropped with the dry weather. However, the open spot might draw in air power, so keep your ears and eyes open."

There is a down grade approaching the water, so the engine makes little noise. The second truck full of wounded is following a short distance behind, cautiously. Bay's vehicle has slowed to a crawl as it enters the water. The bridge is almost at the surface but looks low enough to be fairly invisible from the air. As they climb up the bank off the bridge the second truck enters the water.

"I can hear a plane" yells Chanh. "Hurry, get the hell up the bank."

Bay guns his old truck and makes it to cover on the trail ahead. The second truck is about centered on the river when the fighter drops down, coming in with guns blazing. The truck is hit, heavily sprayed with cannon fire from the attacking aircraft, an A-1E which was the war horse of the VNAF. The truck remains stationary in the middle of the river. No one from Bay's truck is able to reach the riddled transport full of screaming men. The plane makes a sharp turn and comes barreling back with cannons blazing, firing a rocket which nailed the truck broadside. It immediately goes up in flames. The driver springs from the inferno into the water. And that was it. All were lost.

"Back to the truck," Bay screams. Chanh and Hanh have made the waters' edge but turn to rejoin Bay up the bank. "Chanh, help the driver. He's making it out of the river. And hurry. I'll get the truck going."

And that was it. This truckload of wounded men who might have made it back to Hanoi and had a life, were no more.

CHAPTER 7:

_____

DA NANG

I FIND GENERAL LUONG AT HIS HEADQUARTERS SMOKING his ever present British State Express 555 cigarettes, seemingly lost in contemplation. He nods as I enter and motions me over. I don't smoke but have one with him. In Viet Nam it is viewed as impolite to refuse the offer of a gift…so what can you do. We are partners of a sort, after all.

"You like Courvoisier, Capt. Edward?

And I choose to not refuse that offer of friendship either. So, we settle down with a smoke and brandy…and he begins.

"My men leave. They go home. Not good for this war. You know?" he asks.

I reply that certainly I do. That this is not a good omen however not so rare in the history of warfare if one looks closely over the years. A long war, no sudden victory…young men lose their enthusiasm, even the patriots. He began talking of when he was one of those young men, one of the patriots.

General Luong continued: "In fact, when I was young and we Vietnamese were still fighting the French, I favored the Viet Minh while attending high school in Saigon. They were my people. Like so often with the young I was rebellious, as were many of my friends. We were being schooled in Cochin China which had perhaps greater French influence politically than did the northern provinces and our families generally supported the French, mainly because their livings were made working with them or for them. So, you see after school I enlisted in the National Army and attended the Thu Duc Reserve Officer School, our West Point, and here I am today. I remember the dreams of youth but must face the present realities. Maybe not so good."

He smiles, lights another 555 and downs his glass of cognac.

"We must stay in touch Captain Edward Winslow. I am going to Saigon for some meetings. We will talk more when I return. Good day now."

I leave the general and go looking for Jake Barns. He isn't around but I happened to meet up with Len Peters of military intelligence in the mess hall, so we pour more coffee and sit down for a chat. I'm telling him the gist of my conversation with the General.

"Yes, there is more of that, but not so much more. Not from what I'm hearing from my 'sources'.

I smile at that, and he catches me.

"Keep your fucking snickering to yourself, Winslow, I get your drift, but am no fool. It's a long way from all of them deserting, so we stick with it. In a way you can't blame them. Where has the army of their great benefactor gone? Over the hill, right. Back to the 'World'…perhaps where they all should have stayed so many years ago.

I'm thinking about then that I will go and look up Lien, but he isn't thorough.

"Within a couple of weeks something will be happening in the A Shau. That's according to very, very good intelligence…Military Intelligence, if you will and one thing more Winslow, if and when…we've a ticket out. Most of them don't, so try and understand."

"If there's anything that I do understand, it's just that," I reply. "In more ways than one. In fact, you could say my life depends on it."

We part ways and I take the long walk from the airfield to Tran Phu Street. Along the way I remember that Lien is working this morning. An idea enters my mind, so I crossed Tran Phu, then walk along Bach Dang Street till reaching the IVS office. Chi is working at the front desk.

"Is Emerson around, you beautiful thing," I ask her. She looks up and smiles.

"He is in the back working at his desk...and thank you, Captain Ed. Good morning."

I walk out back to Em's office and after greetings and small talk, I ask him about a small, secret pool he once mentioned where he and Chi on occasion visited for a private swim and sometimes...love fest. He grins and motions me towards a seat.

"Now why would you want to visit that place my good friend?"

"You could guess," I answer. "I need to get away with Lien where we lose our regular crowd and can bask in each other's presence. And might even breech the topic."

"This'll work. Take the road over the pass and halfway down the Hue side, hang a left. You'll soon see a path. Walk for a klick or so and the 'secret pool' will suddenly appear before your very eyes. You can't miss it. And by the way, its name is Elephant Springs."

"Thanks Emerson, many thanks. Maybe catch you tonight for a beer."

I bid them both farewell and walk up the street to the Bamboo where I find Lien. Van Ly is nowhere in sight. There are only a couple of customers. ARVN soldiers, officers that I'm not acquainted with. Lien is busy fixing onion omelets, the morning specialty.

"Could you fix me one also Miss Lien?" I asked. Better to keep things professional in present company.

"I can do Captain Winslow, but you must wait your turn."

A copy of Stars and Stripes has been left on the bar, so I take up a corner stool and began reading. Stories are much the same as the past month or so. South Vietnam government running out of money. Need more US funding…also for the military. Congress is in no mood to cooperate. There is more, but nothing new.

Lien finishes with her customers, then serves me the omelet with coffee. She smiles but remains busy behind the bar. I enjoy watching her, this flawless beauty. So busy and serious with an air of innocence. But she is not innocent. She is a survivor in a harsh world and innocence would never have permitted that.

She says that Van Ly should be in for the mid-day shift. I mention that since I'm able to escape for the rest of the day, perhaps she could also.

"Maybe I can. I check with Van Ly when she gets here."

Van Ly appears shortly and agrees to cover for Lien. Maybe she could work later that evening. It is agreed, and we leave for the apartment on Lien's motorbike. I dismount and walk. A 50 Honda doesn't cut it. This required a stop back at IVS where I borrow Emerson's 250 Honda, the big bike in Da Nang. I'd learned on an old Indian Chief, years ago back in Port Kent and haven't ridden regular since, but in this country if you aren't using army transport for any distance you need a motorbike.

In no time we're cruising past Red Beach where the Marines were foolish enough to come ashore back in '65. They'd had a mean, nasty slug ever since. Lien and I sometimes stop at a little stand on this beach for a soda and beer, but not today. We continue on, climbing the treacherous road to the top. The military traffic is light thus far and civilians always pull over this time of day for a snooze, so we crested in no time. Now we're in need of a soda and beer, so stop at the stand across the highway from the old French Pillboxes that are manned by ARVN Marines.

We pull up a stool overlooking the sea where the breeze feels like heaven and enjoy the moment…for a moment. Two ARVN marines approach our spot and rudely asked what I am doing with a Vietnamese woman. My inclination is to answer, 'none of your fucking business,' but I control myself and in almost perfect Vietnamese replied that she was my wife, and that we could do very well without their company. And then I continue.

"Listen soldier, I am an officer in the US Army and expect to be treated as one. Where is your commanding officer? I need to speak with him."

They apologize profusely and say, "no, no, we very sorry. We go now."

Lien thinks that they looked like Saigon Cowboys who have finally been caught up in the Draft and haven't quite shed their old ways. Quite frankly, the local men do not look kindly on foreigners becoming involved with native women. And quite frankly, neither does the American Military Command…especially not officers like me. Going native here is frowned upon nearly to the degree as in old English India. But regardless… we do. We cannot help ourselves.

The trail leaves the pass highway as predicted by Emerson, and the path to the pond is quickly covered. The first view of the pool, the waterfall and the rock cliffs are breathtaking in their own way. A beautiful oasis.

Considering that Lien and I have been lovers for some time, she still exhibits the bashfulness common to all Vietnamese women. She's worn her bathing suit under her clothes. I'm wearing the OD Boxer shorts, so we were a go…a very modest go.

"Oh, the water so cold" Lien said.

For me it's perfect. Almost like a spring fed pond in northern New York, back in the day.

Not that cold, hell no. It was perfect after soaking up the stifling heat that predominates in this country. We settle down and eventually fit in some love making lying in the sun after Lien has warmed herself while I soak in the cool water. And we have a long discussion on our future…which remains inconclusive A great afternoon, far removed from the ever-present war.

It's later and Emerson Fitz and I are having that beer and Lien is back behind the bar. Time for the evening rush at the Bamboo. I haven't seen Jake Barns since he and Banks left for the docks looking for helicopter parts. Omar has disappeared and Peters and Everest haven't been around.

"Well Lien, looks like at the pool. Just you and me….now with our old pal Emerson of course." She smiled her demure smile in my direction and went back to her work behind the bar. Preparations for the evening traffic. Emerson has regressed into his quiet mood. Then Omar shows up.

"Sgt. Omar, how be you? Haven't seen you for a few days. Any action?"

"Too much my Captain. This time we take APCs to Tra My area, then drive north some ways. There is word of NVA scouting team in that sector so we will cut them off from their headquarters in the A Shau. That what we think. We dismount and walk for hour or so. Then as GI say, 'all hell break loose'. We have only small team of twelve men. Young, and not much experience. We hit the ground. Much AK fire We don't know how strong is this force. LT commanding the operation ask me to call in air power. Maybe too soon I think but I can do, as he say. For maybe half hour we trade fire with them I think no side can see the other….just shoot in the direction. When air power come, I am not sure if I can give good fix for bombing. One F 4 comes in low after he has my direction. He miss by mile but NVA stop shooting and disappear so maybe it be ok. I here now. "

He orders a beer from Lien, then Emerson pipes up.

"I'm working with the village in Tra My, because you people have bombed it more than once already. If I go back a few years you've bombed it many times. Looks like I'll take a drive up there tomorrow and see how they're doing. Sounds like the action was some ways from the village but who knows."

I ask Emerson to let it go for the night. Try to escape the real world as we all were trying to do. One day at a time. Then Barns and Banks walk in. This could prove to be a long night. Omar immediately began filling Maj. Barns in on the day's actions.

"I heard about it Omar. You needed me for air cover. I heard the call come in, but Banks was still getting the old machine up and running. Right Banks."

"Right on Major. Tomorrow we can hit it. For now, we drink."

They go back and forth for some time on how different air support might have been helpful, but it seems to me that it all worked out. No one was killed. What could be better.

Then Banks says. "Back in Arkansas this time of night we talk about women."

I'm thinking that females of any age are all Banks ever thinks of, as is the way with most GIs…and some officers. He contains the workings of a Huey in his southern brain when he must. The rest of the time….girls look out.

"Let's drop it considering present company" I ask him.

Lien has heard everything imaginable from these guys, but still…and Omar isn't much better. Then who shows up but Lt. Art Everest, the old Seal and Capt. Len Peters the Psych War expert. This will be a long, long night. I ask Lien if Van Ly is coming back for the late-night shift, and she nods yes.

"One round of 33 for all concerned and that's it until we have some serious discussions on where the hell this war is heading. I've come across some info today that might be of interest to you all," interjects Capt. Peters, "or should be."

So the 33 beer is spread all around and we, all of us, wait for the grand news from military intelligence. No one up here in Da Nang expects much from this source mind you because we've had so much bad info over the last year or so, or perhaps we just ignored it all. Saigon ran the show and for the most part we were aware that they did not 'know fuck all'. However we're open to most anything, and Peters is smiling as he begins.

"This is pertinent…but very low key. A youngish looking guy dressed in ragged peasant garb showed up at my decidedly low-key office yesterday and wanted to give himself up. He said he had heard of the ARVN Chieu Hoi program where safe passage was given to defectors. He said he had valuable information and that was why he came to the MI office. Local people had given him directions. He had no ID but claimed to be a corporal in PAVN stationed in the A Shau."

Omar starts laughing, which is not good. Peters doesn't really know him.

"Watch it Sergeant, I take that as insubordination," is Peters comeback. He looks pissed.

I bud in. I mean Omar is an old friend and something of a patriot. Not much but something.

"You'd better explain yourself Omar." And he does.

"So sorry Capt. Peters, but I be surprised that this chieu hoi can be important source. See many over many years and very few can be trusted. But I glad to listen."

Peters calms down and continues. "I questioned him thoroughly through our interpreter and observed him to be straightforward. You must remember that their agenda may not resemble ours, so to quote you Sergeant Omar 'I be careful' while going through his response. And to be honest none of his report was definite but you have to remember in the intelligence business nothing is definite. It's all about different shades…varying shades of grey. That's why we have experts like me."

He smiles after that last remark which is something considering this guy's regular demeanor. Omar and Banks leave for the pool table apparently having heard enough. Emerson walks out in disgust without a word of farewell.

"Let's get with it Peters" says Barns, "what's going on? Is Giap on his way down the trail?"

"Hardly Major Barns. Let me explain. This kid has only been in the northern army for a little over a year. He's a catholic from Phat Diem, and not very patriotic. Says he wants to go home and become a priest. If any of you remember Greene's 'Quiet American' you'd remember there being a catholic cathedral in that town. But that's neither here nor there. From his listening around camp, he thinks an invasion of the South is imminent. Nothing definite mind you but he swears that he recently saw Le Duc Tho riding south on the trail…on a motorbike, all alone. Probably going to Loc Ninh. He claims higher ups in his unit verified his identity. You can make little of that as most of you probably will….but I have a feeling."

"Jesus Christ, Peters," says Everest. "In my trade we'd never buy it."

"Yes, I get it Arthur, in your trade you'd have cut his throat before he ever made it to MI headquarters. And you'd have learned nothing."

Everest smiles, "We'd have learned just about as much as you have. Le Duc Tho on a motorbike from Hanoi to Loc Ninh. What the fuck man, who'd believe that."

Well, I believe it. I'd heard from a certain bar maid not so long ago that in 1965, soon after the Marines had landed here that a general from the North, possibly Giap himself, had walked right up to the fence surrounding the Air Base dressed in peasant garb, to see for himself just what was going on and just what they'd have to prepare for. The peasant population was faceless and unidentifiable to the Americans. To all Americans, even myself. In a certain sense, they all look the same, as we do to them. Granted, he took a chance, but what's war all about?

"On second thought," said Everest, "perhaps I would believe that story. Two nights ago, on a clear and starlite evening, I was dropped off in the A Shau with five of my men to learn what I could, if anything, about just what you're talking about. Obviously, this portion of the trail doesn't go to Loc Ninh. You've got to stay in Laos till Cambodia and then travel some distance before entering Viet Nam. Your man must have been on the trail above Base 611. Fuck, it. I'll buy it Peters. But what now? Where to from here?"

"Let's have another 33 Art and forget about it till tomorrow. Let's face it, I don't know where the hell it's going. But I can assure you that we will not be here in this bar six months from now. We sure as hell are not going to be here. Why don't you stop in the office tomorrow morning and we can talk."

"I'm up for it," said Lt. Arthur Everest, "where's the beer."

Lien was serving up the bar as he speaks. Van Ly has also just walked in. Somewhat late for her, and she's usually very punctual. I always wonder if she's out visiting with her family, from 'the other side' as she puts it. Be normal enough. That's the story in every country where there's a semblance of civil war. This one's a little different because we don't say it's a civil war, but we definitely are supporting one side and if we were not the civil war would be over. But not at this point. We don't seem to be aware that the French and the Vietnamese settled this issue years ago. In fact, twenty years ago. Remember Dien Bien Phu. We learn very slowly we do.

Next morning I'm back talking with General Luong, for there is always the possibility that he has learned something in Saigon, headquarters being what they are. However, that turned out to not be the case.

"What I expected" he said. "Morale dropping. Short on supplies. Thieu says to hang on, that we can win. I have a family too, and neither I nor they will be viewed kindly by the North if they should come out on top."

What can I say that would help? Hell, I tell him to keep in touch with the US Embassy where he must have some contacts. They all have contacts. That's the name of the game here. And contacts with the other side are not unheard of…and are always suspected.

"I am a friend of Mr. Polgar" he replied after a period of silence. "Next time I travel to Saigon I will look him up."

This surprises me somewhat. I don't know why really, but Tom Polgar is a big shot. He is the CIA Station Chief at the Embassy so General Luong does have a contact there…the best of contacts. I'll keep that in mind.

CHAPTER 8:

THAI NGUYEN

SERGEANT CHANH HAD AN UNEVENTFUL JOURNEY AFTER leaving the catastrophe at the bridge on the Truong Son Trail with Bay and Hanh. He was able to catch rides continuing his journey that were easy and constant. When he left his last ride well into the North, the driver with whom he had become friendly offered him the use of a small motorbike that he kept at the last way station. A price was agreed upon and Chanh is on his way home.

Cruising through Hanoi did not pick up his spirits. Grey, drab, bomb damage…poverty everywhere.

Chanh did not stop, other than gassing up before crossing the Paul Dormer Bridge, the first steel bridge across the Red River that was built by the French and named for the Governor General of French Indochina. This bridge had sustained heavy bombing over the last ten years and while much damage was visible, it had held and was busy with traffic.

The drabness of Hanoi seems to be following along with him as he traveled the highway towards home. He noticed oil drums stored along the way hidden off the road under thatch roofs or vegetation. The attendant who had fixed his flat tire had said that was the way the government had hid their petrol supplies away from the American Bombing which had lessened over the last few years. Seems like what had worked in the worst years of the war was being stuck with. It appeared to him that the population had lost some of its zest for life. Perhaps just war weary like himself.

Chanh arrived in Tan Lap shortly before darkness set in and rode to his family house on the edge of the village farmland. His mother literally passed out when she answered the door, hardly recognizing him, old and skinny as he was. There ensued a family reunion with those still at home. He had become overcome with sadness when told that two of his brothers had died somewhere along the trail. One as a soldier and the younger one as a laborer with the reconstruction teams. His sister Hanh was overjoyed with his appearance which helped him accept his loss. Hanh helped his mother and father in the fields. The rest of the family had spread out beyond the farm.

There was a distance however, behind his brain that he couldn't overcome. Something separated him from this old world and his family, the people that had throughout his life been closest to him. The one constant in all of those difficult years he had been in the South had been the girl Hoa. He was not sure that his memory of her bore any semblance to the present. For too long his real world had been the day to day struggle to survive in a world away from this old home and family that had once been his life.

Chanh did his best to become familiar with his parents and sister. He filled them in partially on his years away. After a simple meal he begged sleep but before crashing he spent time sitting on the front stoop overlooking the fields where he had spent his youth. They were not that different. This area was far enough from Hanoi to have been spared bombing. The stars in the sky and the moon almost let him believe that he'd never left. They were the same. His one worry was, as always, Hoa. Had she kept him in her memory as he had her? Tomorrow would tell.

It is a sunny morning with hardly a breeze as Chanh walks across the fields to the edge of the hamlet where Hoa had lived. He'd made peace with himself after the disastrous evening when he'd heard how his family struggled over the past years. He was moving forward. He couldn't remember just where Hoa did live. So many years ago, and even though things looked familiar the particulars were vague. He enquired at a number of houses and was finally directed to hers. He could see a young woman in front of a thatched roofed house having tea alone. As he walked towards her, she stood up and gazed his way. She stood there as he walked slowly in her direction.

"Chanh, is that you?" she said. "I knew you'd find me somehow. I knew that you couldn't be gone from this earth before we were together, and that we could talk again of a new life."

She rushed toward him then with tears streaming down her face. He had slowed to a stop as she talked not knowing what to do. He also hesitated, unsure of himself, for he'd been in the company of soldiers for far too many years. They then met and embraced, soaked in each other's tears.

Eventually the couple moved to the veranda where Hoa had been when he had arrived. She refreshed the pot of tea, and they sat almost in silence for a time, both not believing they were together and neither knowing what to say. Letters had passed between them during their long period of separation, however delivery was sporadic or nonexistent. A year in transit wasn't unheard of. They were lovers in memory but near strangers in the present. Hoa served them morning pho. It helped. They began talking of their existence over those years of separation.

"I dreamed of you" said Hoa, "for so long a time after you left. There were letters but not many. For more than a year now there had been no word. I was afraid you had been killed. In one way I was afraid to keep on living."

Chanh had nothing to say about those lapses. Everything was beyond his control. Life itself was beyond his control.

"You can't know what I was doing all of those years" he said. "I can't repeat it. But about you Hoa. Tell me about your life here over those lost years."

The sun was rising in the sky, spreading its warmth over the land of Tan Lap. A glorious morning revealed a world neither had foreseen a day earlier. She told him of the earlier years, when her dear sister had left to live with her uncle in Da Nang. And that she had been able to finish school eventually being qualified as a teacher. He asked her about her mother and father.

"My father was killed on a trip to Hanoi three years ago. He was caught up in the American bombing. Not a year later my mother died, I think from sadness. So you see my cousins farm the little bit of land that they had and I teach school in the neighboring hamlet. But I need more Chanh, I need you, a life with you. Can you stay now?" she said.

He explained that he was on a short home leave and would have to head back tomorrow.

"I think that the war could be over in less than a year my dear Hoa. My commander Captain Bao is sure of it. Maybe in half that time. We cannot know but I must return."

"But you've done enough. How many years do they expect you to give of your life?"

"To be truthful Hoa, I believe the war has gone on too long, much too long. Many of us think like that but we cannot freely say so. The political commissars watch. I am no longer a believer. My wish is to be here with you forever. But for now, I cannot leave my friends. Many have died for the country, and we've worked together for so long. I must go back. I can say no more."

"I know" she said, "I know. But I must hope."

They talked for the rest of the morning and Hoa then fixed a small lunch of spring rolls and fresh fruit. They spent the afternoon walking the local fields, saying hello to old friends that they came across, then retreating to Hoa's place. Chanh was thinking that he should return to his family but couldn't bear to leave Hoa. They stayed together talking into the evening.

"You'd better stay the night with me," said Hoa. "We may never have another chance."

Chanh did stay the night, the best of his life. Love making, then tears... knowing that tomorrow would lead to another separation. He was up early and fixed tea. He was thinking that it wouldn't be possible for him to leave for the front immediately. It would not be right to leave her so abruptly. So he stayed for another day. There was no school. They spent part of the time with his family but preferred to be alone together. Their plans were inferred. There was no use talking. Everything would depend on the end of the war.

Another night of love making, then a tearful farewell.

"I will be here for you" she said, "forever," as he mounted the motorbike and began his journey back to the Front.

The skies were clear as Chanh rode down the beginnings of the Truong Son Trail, riding shotgun in a Russian deuce and a half just below its entry to Laos. He'd had an uneventful ride from Tan Lap down past Hanoi to Ban Dupre where the roads merged into the Laotian end of the Trail, and where soon after he'd returned the motorbike to its owner. He was riding along with the driver Dai in the open truck that carried a load of canned goods for the kitchens in the way stations along the highway south. He felt good. He was past his sadness leaving Hoa and was thinking forward to his return when the war ended.

"Do you think it will be over soon?" he asked Dai.

Dai laughed. "I think that for many years, and here I am, driving down the mountain roads south with my load of goods. When I began, I was pushing a bicycle. So this truck is my progress. Maybe it never ends."

"Never say that" said Chanh. "It must end for we all need a life. A real life with wife and children and farm and laughter and food and rice wine. That be all we want...what every man wants."

A few more rides through the night like this and Chanh was back at Base 611 where he checked in with headquarters. After spending the night, he caught a ride back down through the A Shau until meeting up with his unit at their base camp.

"Ah, it is good to see you Sergeant Chanh," said Captain Bao. "I knew you would make a trip very fast. You know you are needed at the front with your platoon."

"To be truthful Chief, I did not want to come back. I want to stay home and marry my girl. I am sick of this war. You know I told you that before."

"And you remember that I told you to keep that kind of thought to yourself. You should talk things over with your three-man cell. It may be advisable for you to have a self-criticism session."

"Yes, I will do that Chief. If they say so I will do. But I do not need self-criticism. I know things. I know myself. For too many years I have been fighting in the South, and I have been thinking."

"How about some tea Sgt. Chanh. Let's take a seat and you can tell me something of your trip North. I have never been to a large city, being from the farm country a little south of Phat Diem. I have never seen Hanoi."

Chanh was more than ready to change the conversation and reminisce with the Chief. Perhaps be a good opportunity to reconnect. It took some time to cover the Truong Son Trail in these modern times for the Chief also hadn't been back since coming down nearly ten years ago. It was hard for him to imagine the change that Chanh described.

"I guess you'd have to realize" the Chief was saying, "that this kind of improvement must have taken place, or we wouldn't have been able to maintain our struggle against the Imperialists. Or those puppet troop bastards we're fighting now."

Chanh nodded and continued with his tale of back with the family and his lover up north in Thai Nguyen. It was during the return on the motorbike when he made a pit stop for gas, food and rest that he wanted to relay an incident that the Chief might find of interest.

"You might find this hard to believe Chief, but I tell you it's true."

"Go ahead, don't keep me waiting. And it better be good."

He began by saying that he'd had to pull over several kilometers above Ban Dupre for a pit stop. After checking the bike over and fueling it up, he pulled up a stool at a nearby pho stand for noodles and tea. Maybe even a beer if they had any.

"I was talking up the girl who ran the stand hoping that she could find me a beer after finishing up with the meal. She smiled, and I took that as a positive. There were a couple of guys that walked up and sat across from me. They were loud and fat, so it was obvious that they were political functionaries. I hadn't seen a fat person in years. Not up in Thai Nguyen either. That's what made me sure of it. Well believe it or not, they began making fun of Ho Chi Minh who is, as we all know, a saint to every Vietnamese. Immediately I began thinking, what the fuck are they talking about? Are they looking to get their asses kicked? But I kept still. They continued talking about the masses of mankind and how they live off them. In point of fact, what suckers these masses were. I took it as what a sucker I was. And I wasn't alone. There were other soldiers around, plus any number of travelers or farmers or whoever, but they were all dressed in almost rags and certainly not fat. Almost starving some of them looked like. Well fuck those fat assholes. I lit into them bad. Told them that they were traitors to our class struggle, not to mention defending the country from foreign and puppet soldiers. Not to mention the sacrilege committed against Uncle Ho."

The Chief was astonished. He couldn't believe it and kept rushing Chanh to continue his story.

"You can believe I got right in their face. I wasn't afraid of those bastards. Told them I'd been fighting for nearly ten years in the South and you assholes are living it up as if you were in Paris while we 'the masses' suffer and do all the work and the fighting. Some other guys, and girls too, gathered around. They started cheering me. Made me proud and I kept it up. The fat guys were looking worried and began shouting back at me. Saying if I knew who they were I'd never say a word. I said I'd do more than say a word. I'd kick their asses…both of 'em. Then I nailed one right in the face, the fattest one. He yelled and one of the girls started pulling his hair and kicking him. The other one was trying to get the hell out. Then a problem. A policeman showed up, so I backed off. The political guy intimidated the cop, and he started going through the crowd looking for the troublemaker that had accosted these very important politicians. I got it… right quick. Turned back to my motorbike, kicked it over and sped off going like hell. And that's the last I heard of that incident. Pretty good Chief, don't you think."

The Chief agreed with Chanh, his able sergeant. He was very proud of him.

"Good for you Sergeant Chanh. Here, have some more tea. Then I'll fill you in on the happenings around here since you've been gone."

Capt. Bao went over the time when Chanh was in the North, which appeared to have been rather uneventful. Aside from a few skirmishes with the puppet troops, mostly quiet. Waiting. Chanh wanted to get back to his men and talk things over with them. He let the chief finish then took his leave saying he had to square himself and his pack away in the bunker where he lived with his platoon. Privates Cuong and Huu were sitting out front talking away, as was their want, when Chanh approached. They enthusiastically welcomed him.

"Ah, Sgt. Chanh, we missed you," said Huu. " Tell us of your trip. And all about your girlfriend."

So Chanh went over his trip with these guys too. It's necessary, for most of them would not be going anywhere. It picked up morale to hear of someone who was able to break the chains of control to move back into the real world, if only for a short time. They wanted to hear everything. Where he went, who he saw, how things were with his family…and most especially everything about his love life. And so it went.

CHAPTER 9:

DA NANG AIR BASE

JAKE BARNS AND I ARE HAVING COFFEE AT ONE OF THE shops run by the local girls a short distance from headquarters on Da Nang Airfield. It looks like a slow day, but who knows? I haven't seen him for few days and am wondering if he'd been out on any operations or medivacs.

"So what about it Jake...slow day coming up?" And that was it for starters.

"Are you a fucking joker or what?" he replied. "It's never a slow day here...unless you make it one."

That left us both laughing like hell until Jake got down to business. "Is there any way I could crack that Van Ly. Man, I love her. And she's got some size to her. You know, big enough to wrap your legs around. And she's so smart."

"Where the hell did that come from? And I don't think you can. She's mysterious. And she's more than once mentioned that she has family 'on the other side'. Of course, they all probably do, however she might have a husband 'on the other side'. Who knows? No Jake, I don't think you are ever going to 'wrap your legs' around her. I think she's too smart for that. Never happen GI, as Banks would put it."

"You're lucky Ed. You found Lien. Me, I've never been lucky with women…or girls for that matter. Not even in the States. Christ, I was a top cadet at Norwich and couldn't even nail a Vermont milk maid. And man, there were some lookers on the local dairy farms. How's that for being a total failure?"

"Well," I begin, "did you ever try for a part time job milking cows on one of those farms. That might have worked. Any farm girl worth a damn would have gone for a guy that could milk a cow before some jar head from the local college. And you've got to remember that the hip scene was coming along when we were at school and guys in the military were mostly considered suckers, not heroes. No man, you should have learned to milk cows."

"I'll tell you something Captain Edward Winslow, no self-respecting, top of his class cadet in one of the nation's top military schools would stoop to milking cows. Let's have a little respect."

"Hey, I was talking about getting a hold of some sexy, pretty girls. You do whatever it takes my friend, you know that."

"Listen, I have my pride….or I had my pride. Right about now I'd do anything to get my hands on Van Ly. No, that's not right. Too crude. I'd do whatever it took to have her want to genuinely make love with me. How's that?"

"Very good, but to get back to the cows. You know Jake, I have cousins up north that milked cows. I don't know how they stood it actually. I mean there's a whole large world out there beyond the farm… but then something happened. Back to the earth. The farm scene turned hip and the hippie chicks showed up. So, milking could have paid off double for you. Too bad you missed it."

I'm being over the top but anything to escape the reality of Viet Nam in the first months of 1975. Things weren't looking good, and we were losing momentum.

"To move on Ed, how about a short flight in my Huey? Banks just finished a 20 hour inspection and wants to take it up for a check ride. And it's a beautiful morning so let's take an aerial tour of the local countryside. We'll loop around Monkey Mountain first because I want to check a few spots out that looked suspicious to me last time I flew over it. You know it's said that we never had absolute control of that piece of real estate. A little like the Black Virgin near Tan Ninh down south. We held the top and the bottom, but never the middle. Right now they've probably got the whole damn thing and it's nearly within the city limits."

"Maybe you're right Jake. Sure, I'll go along. The weather's right for it." I wanted to ask him about General Luong but that could wait. We walk along towards the ramp where Banks is finishing up with his inspection.

"Five minutes and we're set to go Major," said Banks. who was all business when not out drinking or chasing women.

We're cruising along at 500 feet or so heading south over the paddy lands towards Marble Mountain. The beautiful greens of Viet Nam raised my mood and eliminated thoughts of the ongoing war. What a beautiful morning. Barns banks the machine left and we circle over the shops that carved the marble statues that give the mountain its name. There are always rumors that money from this trade was being siphoned off by the VC, but this kind of thinking originated with the GIs and was applied to most every money making endeavor. Definite proof always seemed to be lacking. I'm wearing a helmet that was plugged into the Huey's radio net to stay in touch with Barns.

"Ok Captain, now we will head up north over China Beach and check out the monkeys on Monkey Mountain. I don't mean the real monkeys. I mean the 'red' monkeys."

I laughed to myself. He could be full of shit sometimes. I check the beach out as we drop down to less than a hundred feet staying over the water. The glory days of the GI R and R center are long gone. The only people using this old pleasure piece of gorgeous sand are fisherman pulling in drag nets toward the shore. No Vietnamese has time to take off and go swimming in the middle of the morning. They're too busy trying to stay alive. As we approach the mountain peninsula Barns climbs the machine back up to 500 feet where we're able to view something other than the shoreline. Vegetation is so thick that realistic visibility isn't going to happen. And it looks as if someone on the ground wouldn't fare much better. Way too much green.

"Barns, let's gain some altitude and check out the site of the old Signals Intelligence base that was moved to Thailand. I think it's empty now."

We level off a little more than two thousand feet and circle the top where some antennas still exist but certainly do not look operational. The buildings a bit lower down appear to have been stripped. There's no evidence of use. We don't land, just drop down the other side and fly over the Navy piers and back to the airbase.

The flight takes less than a half hour and we soon end up talking it over in the mess hall.

"Nothing there," says Barns. "Not even a monkey... either kind." And he laughs like hell one more time.

"I think I'll run that by Everest. I bet you his Seal Team, or part seal team or whatever the hell he runs has been up there."

"Well, here he comes," replies Barns, "go get him."

Lt. Arthur Everest is an odd guy, or should I say officer. A very strict officer in the main but lately he is running ragged. A little warn down per-haps. Actually, that could be good for a Seal out in the boonies, but noticeable for an officer on the base...or in the bars for that matter. In a strange way though he never did really give a damn for anything but the important basics. Appearances could wait.

"Well Lt. Everest... Art, how's it going this morning... noon I guess it is." Barns and I were just talking about you. We took a flight around Monkey Mountain...checking it out."

"Well, I'll tell you guys one thing. You're lucky you didn't get your machine shot down. There's no heavy stuff up there but ground fire can be lethal if you fly close to the surface."

"What are you taking about? No evidence of ground fire. Everything looked peaceful. I tell you we neither saw nor heard anything."

"Like I was saying boys, luckier than hell. My team is up there on occasion. And so aren't the 'boys'. If it was me, I'd keep a platoon on top where the old signals intelligence base was. The buildings are still serviceable, after a fashion. I think the VC are left off along the shoreline on the lee side out of site on moonless nights from sampans. You think about it, it's much easier than slugging your way through that thick jungle up there. My guess is they use the old antenna sites at the peak for observation posts."

"Well, I don't know what they're going to see from up there," I said. "All I can say is we saw nothing and heard nothing and there was no evidence of any presence at all. Didn't even see a monkey." He smiled at that one. But not Everest.

Lt. Everest grins a little and comes back with this. "We shot a couple of VC up there less than a week ago. and they weren't green kids. We couldn't figure out what the hell they were doing. They were camping near the old buildings down below the antenna at the peak, not using the buildings. They had no papers on them. Not even ID, so we figured there must be something going on. I think they were just routine spies keeping track of things from the peak that overlooks this whole area. Even the port. Good close view of that considering. Probably prepping for the finale."

I thought I'd pop a little info into old Arthur with this.

"Did you know Arthur, that General LeRoy Manor commanded the raid on the Son Tay POW camp up North from that site. They brought in special equipment just for that operation. Apparently, most of what they needed was already installed and the site had the perfect elevation to manage the whole shebang."

Everest grins and comes back with this. "Do you think I'm a fucking idiot. Of course, I know all about that raid and how it used this site for overall communication. I've worked with Roy Manor at times and know him quite well."

"Ok Arthur, you've got me there. What else?"

"As far as up there goes, all is in the dark. We have however… we think we have turned up something in the A Shau near the old Special Forces Camp."

He goes on how his team, I gather Seal team, for he's not been that clear about his goings on or with whom, but they were out there. Actually, he isn't that clear on just what they saw but apparently it's very suspicious.

"I want to know who the fuck you flew out there with," interjected Barns. "Why wasn't I called?"

"Ask the bosses," said Everest. "I don't have a free hand here, not these days. The fucking gooks are in charge. That's why things look so promising."

Let's just say that didn't go over well. There has always been an undercurrent of not really racism, at least not with everyone, but a feeling, possibly of superiority. These guys are a bit smaller in stature and they do at times walk around holding hands with each other but so what. Let's face it, they're not white…or black. Some of the black guys, not all certainly, are about as bad as the whites on this issue. Barns looks shocked.

"Arthur, you're talking about half of my crew. They're great guys. Keep that crap to yourself. There's no room for it this stage of the game. The old army has gone home, and these guys are our partners and are what's keeping this replacement for the old time 'green machine' going. If you get my drift."

"Sorry old man, it slipped out. Don't get bent all out of shape. It won't happen again. I wasn't serious. Just slipped it in to see what kind of response there'd be."

"Well, you found out. You pull that shit with some of these younger men that are already showing signs of a grudging attitude and you might get more than your ass kicked. No, probably not you, being a Seal, the toughest of the tough. Perhaps a knife or a bullet let loose that brains and muscle won't stop."

"I get it Barns. Let it go please. Let me get back to what I'm good at."

The story from the A Shau is similar to the killings on Monkey Mountain. Nothing clear there either, however it felt different. They'd come upon another small patrol that shouldn't have been there. Killed one and the rest melted into the jungle. Too tough, even for a Seal Team. Same thing, no Id or other papers. Neither insignia nor indication of rank. This was unusual for NVA troops which these appeared to be.

Everest continues a dissertation that something was up. But we know that. We're aware that the NVA have controlled this turf since the 1st Cav had pulled out in '68 which was a hell of a long time ago in military strategic terminology. We know something's up but just not what nor when.

"It's getting on boys." This late in the night from Van Ly.

Somehow as on so many nights in Da Nang I am back at the Bamboo expecting Lien to show up for a nightcap. She was taking some night classes in English to learn a more precise version than what she now possessed. Barns has just shown up and we're having some light banter with Van Ly. There are some ARVN GIs playing pool in the rear overlooking the riverside deck. Most of these troops have difficulty handling their drink so the tempo is rising. So far their tempers haven't risen above normal levels.

"Van Ly, you look so beautiful tonight, how do you do it?" Barns is saying.

"I do it every day and night Maj. Barns. I be born that way. You get my drift?" She laughs at that and turns back to the bottles to mix us Old Fashions.

"What kind of whiskey you like? Have Jim Bean, Ten High, Early Times…"

"Early Times" I say. "Where did that come from? It's my favorite but I wasn't able to locate it in the PX for the last couple of months."

She laughs…scornfully so and replies. "You be number ten fool Captain Winslow. Next time you check with Van Ly, and I can buy for you. Only charge small finder's fee."

I smile and reply, "no Van Ly, I'm good with anything. Just be sure you have some bitters back there and all will be fine. If you've got cherries so much the better."

"I have cherry" she answers slyly. "You no can have."

Barns and I let that go. Too common for us officers. She did have the fixings and made a more than adequate old fashioned. We sit and sip for a spell in silence. The morning flight is in our mind and puzzling, more so after our talk with Art Everest. We begin going over it eventually. You can see that Van Ly is listening in.

"Don't worry about that now. When it be happening, you will know."

"Yes, but it would be great if we could know just a little bit in advance," I come back with. "That's what we are paid the big money for."

There is nothing else on that subject, so Barns begins his flirting but isn't doing a hell of a lot better than he did with the farm girls back in Vermont when he was a student at Norwich. I tell him to just act normal. Not at all like he's talking to a girl in a bar in Viet Nam.

"Pretend you are in New York, Jake. You'd be surprised sometimes how a local girl in any country can be as sophisticated as one of your polished chicks from a Fifth Ave Co-Op."

He starts over like he imagines a quiet local boy might, and she responds in kind. You've got to remember the two of them have had a long relationship as bar girl and GI which is not very personal. Then lucky for me my former bar girl, girlfriend Lien shows up, and I can leave them be. She fills me in on her English class and indicates that she'd like us to get back to our little love nest and I am in no position to refuse, nor would I wish to.

"Say Barns, let's meet up in the mess for coffee in the morning. Any luck General Luong will be there. Maybe Everest too, and we can have a policy chat if you will."

He smiles at that and nods without breaking his conversation with Van Ly . I'd ridden along with Barns in his jeep to the bar, so Lien and I enjoy the warm night and have a pleasant walk back to our abode on Tran Phu. I would say that on that walk once again the topic came up on when or how or where we would go together, if this whole thing falls in. Once again, we did not come up with any definite plan. I realize that for me it is a no brainer. I do rather love my life in Viet Nam. Once she and I became a couple however, for myself there will be no problem leaving. The world is at my feet. It's likely that we'd move back in the vicinity of Port Kent in New York, or possibly Albany or wherever. Hell, I had a law degree.

Then there was the farther out plan that Lien I think liked the best. We'd head off to Australia as pioneers of old and just see where it went. That too held great promise. There would be no problem with entry to that country either for my friend John Sanderson who works in the Australian Embassy in Saigon had indicated more than once that he could 'fix' the papers. That would not be an issue. At any rate between Lien and myself, our plans remain fluid.

The stumbling block is her leaving Viet Nam, her country. To a great extent she has lost contact with her family, mostly due to the dislocation caused by the war. She has not given up on reconnecting with them. To head out into the great world with me was somewhat beyond her comprehension. Her thinking is that that kind of decision would be too final. She might never again see her country. Certainly I understood that. The better solution at the moment is to jump into bed and let the future go where it may. And that we do; the result being a most memorable night.

I'm once again nursing a coffee early in the mess when Barns walks in.

"Man, I'm hungry. Need more than coffee."

"Ok" I mumble, "get your coffee and refill mine and I'll get the eggs. What's your style? I'm for over easy."

"Scrambled. Loose if you can get it."

The army, not the ARVN, run this mess and I'm friends with Sgt. Maldonado, the ration man who is on the grill this morning. He told me once that the reason he cooked eggs in the morning was that the grill posed such a challenge. He'd always keep at least a dozen pairs of eggs on the grill. Some over easy, some sunny side up, some scrambled. If cheese was available cheese omelet and always Spanish omelet If he was on his game, the line never stopped, which I'd always found was absolutely amazing.

"Sgt. Maldonado my friend, how about those two, that over easy and the scrambled beside it. Can you keep it loose? "

"Sure as hell can, sir, here you go, and there's plenty of bacon next tray down. Keep it moving though. Let the line stop and you'll ruin my morning."

You can damn well bet I didn't let it stop. The line kept moving and Barns and I had eggs as we preferred. Sgt Maldonado was able to forge into his day in great form. Good to know that the army isn't completely fucked up.

"Ok Jake let's get down to business. Anything going on the next few days that I should know about?"

"You're the one that said the general would be here. Be nice to have an off the cuff conversation with him. No…I'm not loaded with any new knowledge, and that is for sure."

"Well get ready, here he comes."

We stand and greet General Luong. In the past he has had to put up with insolence from various American officers… because he is a Vietnamese. A General no less, but Vietnamese. This kind of thing seems to be a sickness within the human race, rather is a sickness that afflicts the whole of humanity so it's a struggle to keep an even keel at times. General Luong is a proud man, more capable than many a US counterpart, and a patriot.

"Good morning to you both," said General Luong. "I would join you for eggs but have already had my bowl of pho down in the market. I love the market in the morning. It lets me take the pulse of my country. It is the heart of my country, and this morning I fear for it."

I go to fetch him a coffee while he sits down and begins talking with Barns.

"The word from Saigon is ambivalent. In some ways I respect President Thieu, however he has become too indecisive. A general, which he was before becoming president, needs to be informed and he needs to be sure of himself ,certainly. When he plans or gives a final order, he needs to exude decisiveness to his subordinates. I do not see that from him presently. I did not hear that on the phone with him earlier this morning. Makes me worry."

"Well General, I certainly am sympathetic to your predicament, but is there anything new that we should know? Any new intelligence?"

"I think not at the moment, but I have this feeling. I need to talk with your Intelligence man Captain Peters and was hoping that he might be here."

"I believe he will General. Let's talk breakfast talk until he shows up. How is your family doing?"

"Everything is fine for now. But I have to prepare."

I mentioned that he had once told me that he was a friend of Tom Polger the CIA Station Chief in the Embassy and wondered if he had anything new or if he had any helpful information if it became necessary to evacuate himself and his family from the country. He said little and indicated little in the way of specifics. Then luckily Captain Peters walks in. He's usually a quiet guy.

"Good morning, General…gentleman. Good start to the day I see. Let me grab some eggs and a coffee and I'll join you."

He sits down with us and eats quickly. General Luong quizzes him on the usual means of his trade. He thinks for a moment, then begins.

"First the A Shau. We have a very limited number of photo interpreters that were trained at Fort Holabird left working with us. Your men that have taken over are good, but due to the terrain in the valley, it is difficult to pinpoint exact locations from the photos that the jets are bringing back. I'm not sure why. I spent two years with the 1st MI and worked at Tan Son Nhut where it seemed we had much better results than we're getting here. We've got trucks spotted along the highway through the middle of the A Shau. They have to have depots and resupply through there in some places. We know that and quite frankly it doesn't mean much. We're looking for troop movements. That's what's missing."

"You'd think it would be impossible to hide the numbers required to make any kind of advancement on this area." I pipe in with. "You've got to be talking many thousands."

"Let me say what I think." It's General Luong. "Too early. This will come very quickly. I think troops are spread all over the Truong Son route to the South and that many are in the mountains in Laos. Supplies have been laid up over the past year and they are well hidden. We need to have information from our men on the ground. I have been working with the Seal team of Lt. Everest on this. They are out there now I believe."

That's news to Barns and me, as we keep in regular contact with Art Everest, not to mention drinking half the nights away with him in the Bamboo. Apparently, he'd reported nothing of any importance thus far, and the General is not forthcoming with any additional intelligence.

Peters continues, "Let's move on closer to home. We know what the Seal team turned up on Monkey Mountain. We have locals posted along the coast at the base of the mountain and periodic drop-offs are made of men and supplies from sampans from up the coast, or so I believe. We haven't been able to pinpoint their departure points. My guess is that they are relayed down the coast from the North on the darkest nights and … there you have it." said Peters.

"You've got C-47s flying over the trail twenty-four/seven, listening in on radio traffic from all of their nets. There must be something there," says Barns. "There have been a few times I've heard something on my helicopter radio set that wasn't ARVN. My gunner Cpl. Doan heard it too and he thinks it must have been some kind of Vietnamese code."

"I can't have an opinion on that," said Peters. "I did get a report from Cham Island spies yesterday that sampans have been spotted dropping off supplies and soldiers on their shores too, in the dark of night. We have no idea what they'd be out there for."

"I can say that any NVA on Cham Island would be preparing for a raid on the Marine base just below My Khe Beach" puts in General Luong, "Maybe… we keep an eye open on that island. I'll tell the Navy to look into it."

And so the conversation went back and forth along these lines with no clear, definite answers on how, what, when or where an NVA incursion could happen. General Luong did indicate once again that he had been in touch with Polgar, but was coasting momentarily. He bids us farewell and leaves for his command post, saying he'd be back in Saigon soon for more meetings.

Len Peters starts reminiscing about his posting with the 1st MI in Saigon some years earlier.

"The battalion was beginning to wind down its operation in RVN and my job was to fly around to our various outposts to help transfer the mission over to the ARVN. Their photo interpreters had been training and working for some time alongside ours so there wasn't that much to it. I hung out with a girlfriend for a couple of months after wrapping that up, then made my exit. I'm not sure why, but the photo interpreters aren't turning up that much lately. Don't mean to blame them. Doesn't look as if they're getting that much to work with."

"Let's get on with day to day living." I put in. "It could be a month, It could be six months. Maybe something will be worked out. Who the hell knows?"

Omar had been eating on the over side of the mess with his marines and comes over to say hello when he sees me. I brief him on the conversation with the General and Peters.

"It be soon," was his reply.

CHAPTER 10:

THE ARVN & THE NVA

A BATTLE HAS BEEN SIMMERING A FEW KILOMETERS EAST of the A Shau, on a ridge and below the ridge, with few open spaces. Sergeant Chanh's unit is been out on a patrol picking their way east to see if they'll run into any opposition. On the second day out, they take some sporadic small arms fire after the mid-day rice break. One man is seriously wounded and two of his comrades are carrying him back to the base camp where he'll be trucked to a way station equipped with a medical clinic. After that incident they're slowly cutting their way forward and continue at that pace till darkness begins setting in where they bivouacked for the night. Privates Cong and Huu are on the last shift of perimeter guard where they sit up on an ambush till dawn brakes. They've been especially cautions during the previous two hours since these were the hours when the enemy normally attacked.

They have joined with their fellow soldiers along with Sgt. Chanh for morning tea and whatever else they could scrounge up for food. They've eaten nothing but rice and nuoc mam the previous evening.

"Sergeant Chanh, what for food. We walk all day yesterday and need some fuel," says Huu who is the funny guy of the platoon.

The PAVN soldier normally carried his tube of rice with him. The main force might or might not be able to provide him with more complete sustenance. Most units have an able bodied soldier who is familiar with the flora and fauna of the jungle and is able to scrounge enough to keep a healthy diet going. Not much, but enough.

"Private Huu, how would we have been able to search the jungle for food yesterday. Under rifle fire? Not very easy. Tea and rice this morning. We will begin a hard day's march very soon and if we come up with nothing, will begin the trek back to our base camp."

"But Sgt. Chanh, I will be so hungry by then I cannot walk. You will have to carry me."

The other troops laugh at that. Sgt. Chanh joins in also for he knows that the men need some easing up, some humor, anything to keep them going. He knows it's a hard push for the men, but for him this was a rather easy day and night. In the ten years he's been on this operation to free the South, hardship is the norm. Sleeplessness is the norm. Exhaustion is the norm. His new replacements have no conception of those previous long years.

"Pvt. Huu, I will not carry you. I will kick your ass all the way to Saigon if I hear one more negative comment."

The men don't know if they should take that comment seriously or laugh. Most of them choose to smile and say nothing. Just drink the tea and eat the rice as slowly as they can to stave off the hunger. The best way, if they have time, is to let the rice soak in their mouth till it mostly dissolves.

"Sgt. Chanh," said Pvt. Huu. "I can't let the rice soak in my mouth. I too hungry. I swallow as soon as I taste."

The bantering goes on for a short time, then the platoon joins up with their main unit and continues the march east. Sgt Chanh's platoon is in the lead where it's hard to ascertain position, for there are numerous foot trails through the heavily forested terrain. The complete company does not stick with just the one track for it would be strung out a kilometer or so and hardly be defensible. The first hour goes quietly. The company is nearing the top of a knoll where there are open spaces of varying sizes. The wop, wop, wop of a Huey helicopter is heard in the distance. Sgt. Chanh gives the order for his men to spread on either side of the trail, take cover and remain hidden till a scout can be sent forward to see what's going on.

"Pvt. Cong," said Chanh, "make your way forward under cover and observe. Do not engage the enemy or make the slightest move that will reveal your position. I might add, our position."

Pvt. Cong obeys his Sgt. and begins the slow movement towards open spaces where helicopters will likely settle in. He wearily approaches the edge of an opening where he can have a view of the open sky and sees four Hueys approaching, still at altitude. Suddenly one of then drops to the ground, in pieces. Another one windmills to a landing that looks survivable. The other two land nearby. Pvt. Cong quickly returns to his platoon to inform Sgt. Chanh.

"I saw four helicopters Sgt. and one crashed for sure and one other was damaged, but I think landed intact. They must have flown into each other. Two others came in safely near the crash site."

"Good for you Private Cong. We will now move forward and observe. We will only engage the troops if it appears that we have an edge. Pvt. Cong, you locate the rest of the Company and relate what you've told me to Capt. Bao. Tell him we have moved forward to the edge of the clearing near the top of the ridge just east of his position. Report back to me when you are able."

Eventually the remainder of the Company joins up with Sgt. Chanh's platoon and observes the ARVN exiting their helicopters and taking up defensive positions. Two helicopters rise up and leave the area. One remains on the ground, probably the command machine. A white man is visible beside the Huey, talking with some ARVN. After a few minutes he boards the machine, and they too climb out to the East.

CHAPTER 11:

THE BATTLE

THE DAY BEGINS AS A TRAINING, SCOUTING EXERCISE. WE have four choppers to work with and manage to pack in forty ARVN Marines. Barns is flying his old reliable, and the other three are manned by ARVN crews. I'm in Barns' machine and Omar is in the follow up. He is going to stay on the ground for contact with air support or dust off if any is needed. I intend to remain with Barns after we have off loaded our troops. We are flying along fifteen hundred feet or so, approaching the A Shau. The intended LZ a few miles East, is quickly coming into view. As we are letting down one of the marines who is riding the skids begins yelling. I looked behind us and see one Huey dropping down wrong side up. No chance of any survivors. An apparent midair. The other has lost his tail rotor and gear box. The pilot seems to have regained control after one windmilling turn, by dropping the nose and picking up enough forward speed to keep it straight. It looks as if he is going to make the clearing. He does, and is able to slip in for a safe landing. The troops on board are able to deplane and join the others. Barns drops in alongside, while Omar's bird skids to a stop behind us. I let the marines I'm with finish unloading. Half have jumped clear before we touch the ground.

Omar and I find ourselves beside each other as all of the marines have moved forward to find cover.

"I must go with my men, Captain Winslow. You monitor my radio net and relay for me any request for air support that I am able to broadcast. Can do Captain?" requests Omar.

I tell him that I will certainly do that and to get his ass moving, keep it down and not to get hurt this late in the game. Gunfire is erupting as Barns lifts off. I'm sitting with my feet on the skid but decide to play it safe and climb back inside where I can fasten in with a seat belt. I contact Barns on the radio after plugging my helmet into circuit.

"Stay local Barns, they might be needing us".

He replies that that is his intention. He's going to circle the area wide and see what happens. In short order green tracers ae visible coming from the tree line. Orange ones are traveling toward it. The green is vastly outnumbering the orange, which does not bode well for our marines…or for Omar. I contact Barns on the radio.

"I see what's going on," he answers, "and I'm going to swing around close to the tree line and have Banks spray the hell out of those fuckers with his M-60."

I hang on as he banks sharply, letting down instantaneously to a couple hundred feet. He races by while Banks opens up, however the return fire is too intense for another pass. We're very lucky.

"Never again with that one," Barns interjects. "I'll climb back up and make a large circle till we see what's happening or until we get called back in. You should contact the other Huey and have him remain on this station also. We may have to medivac some wounded as well as any survivors."

It's too distant by far to make that call, or judgement. This could be a minor skirmish, or it could become a massacre. I'm hoping for the best.

CHAPTER 12:

─────────────

ON THE GROUND

CAPTAIN BAO HAD REGAINED CONTROL OF HIS COMPANY as it regrouped in somewhat close proximity to the tree line overlooking the upper ridge clearing where the ARVN marines had landed. Gunfire was picking up and it looked as if they would get the best of the puppet troops with their return fire.

Sgt. Chanh watched as the two helicopters met in midair with one falling immediately to the ground and bursting into flames. The other managed to make if in for a landing, followed the other two which appeared to be unscathed. He scanned the sky for more, but none came into view. He is mentally computing just how many puppet troops his unit would be fighting and thought not more than thirty or so.

"I think Private Huu," who is at his side, "that we will be able to take charge of this battle. They have only two helicopters left that are serviceable and only one has returned to flying overhead. It is not a gunship so we should have no worries on that score. Just door gunners which makes firing capacity two M-60s. We can win this."

Sgt. Chanh's platoon has taken the lead and is closest to the ARVN force. Capt. Bao walked through the undergrowth to talk with him. They decide to stay with the tree line for the moment and return heavy fire towards the enemy soldiers.

"Let them come towards us," said Captain Bao. "They are bound to suffer some casualties and when they look weakened, we will advance toward them carefully. We must save our soldiers for the final offensive."

Sgt. Chanh smiles to himself after hearing that last remark. He's been told of the final offensive for so long he no longer believes in it. But for now, the errand at hand.

One of his men stood up behind him for a better view and is immediately hit in the face by enemy fire. One man down with no hope. One more young man who will not make it back to the farm. Chanh tries to help but to no avail. He begins to boil in anger. He signals his men forward to take it out on the enemy force. Half remain in the tree line to provide covering fire while the other half low crawl forward, some throwing grenades ahead of them, the others keeping up rapid AK fire support. What has been something of a stalemate begins to crack. Capt. Bao moved in his two other platoons, one on each side of Chanh's.

The ARVN marines have been kneeling for better visibility and firing at their NVA opponents from that level, but it's dangerous. Many have fallen. It begins to be evident that this is not going to be an ARVN victory. Retreat is the only option, and they began pulling back.

Capt. Chanh can sense victory when he suddenly sees two helicopters flying low, heading directly for his position. He signals his men, and they all drop down, hugging the earth. The choppers suddenly land with door gunners spraying the area with fire. Some of his men in the forefront are hit.

CHAPTER 13:

—————————

ARVN MEDEVAC

BARNS CIRCLES HIS HUEY AROUND THE BATTLE POSITION twice then indicates to me that he's heard from the other bird that had found a landing zone nearby and had set down to conserve fuel. It was either that or return to Da Nang to fill up, for if they circle too long, they won't be able to make the return trip and they know they'll be needed to extract the marines at some point… alive, wounded or dead. I relay the situation to General Luong back at headquarters. He's already ordered a Bird Dog from Marble Mountain towards our position to act as airborne radio support for Barns, and myself on the ground as well as to General Luong. Barns has shut down his machine and we are sitting on board with our feet on the skids beside Banks who is still in position behind his M-60.

"Whenever we climb out of here," said Banks, "fly back down that tree line and I'll spray the hell out of those bastards. Got plenty of ammo left."

"Maybe," Barns answers, "but it depends. If an immediate extraction is required, you'll have to shoot from a distance, though I must admit they're not that far apart. It's a fairly narrow ridge but the extraction is what matters. I'll land with you facing the tree line and you'll be able to fire at will."

'Right on Major, I'll be ready."

My radio crackles, and I answer, "Come in."

"Bird Dog 46 Whiskey overflying your operation. It's not going well… looks bad. You should get your birds in the air and come in for extraction. There are many wounded and dead. I've called for a gunship from General Luong. There was only one operational and he's going to send it this way."

I'm sure I recognize the voice from earlier times in the South during the late Sixties. A very distinctive voice.

"Is that you Hank," is my return.

"Winslow… you still here," he comes back with.

It threw me for a loop. This is Hank Sleet's third war. I knew him earlier when he had been flying Bird Dogs as the Air Liaison Officer for the 173rd Airborne that was headquartered at the Bien Hoa Air Base. We'd have to get together later and catch up after this fiasco is wrapped up.

Barns is back on the net as we fly in for a medivac pickup. On reaching altitude I hear from Omar. He says it's bad, but he'll pop smoke so Barns will know the safest spot to land. The other chopper will come in behind us.

Hank is back on the net from his Bird Dog, "Word from Da Nang is the gunship is on its way, but you'll have to attempt pickup earlier. The interpreter will pop smoke where you should set down. Good luck."

Nearing the landing, I try to compute how many soldiers we could safely load in these machines and make it off the ground. We've dropped in thirty or so with three machines and had two to get them out. It'll be tight. Then I can see green smoke. It was agreed ahead of time that green would be used for medivac. If the enemy pops the same our man will pop a quick red. That'll be the spot to land.

Barns comes in fast and pivots as he settles down so Banks will be facing the enemy with his M-60 full face. Dangerous for Banks but the most effective position to protect the troops loading up. The other gunner on the back side is firing down the ridge toward visible NVA.

After landing I leap from the skid and wave to the troops that are running towards us full speed. They're dragging two bodies. Three wounded are being carried by their mates and a number of walking wounded are following.

"Move you bastards," I yell. There's not a second to spare. Omar is the last man remaining on the ground and he's carrying another wounded over his shoulder. I can see the other Huey slowly lifting off, moving forward to gain enough lift to clear the vegetation.

"Fuck me Captain, I'm hit," screams Banks. I turn quickly and see him grabbing his shoulder. We've loaded fifteen. I expected to ride the skid along with Omar but seeing Banks being inoperative, I squeeze in beside him in and take over the machine gun, firing madly at the NVA who are charging the chopper firing as they run. Barns was having trouble lifting off. He rams the machine forward while barely off the ground hoping to gain enough lift to clear the trees. He's having trouble leaving ground effect as the trees get closer.

I've taken Banks' helmet for commo and can hear Barns yelling to who I did not know, "We're not going to clear the fucking trees."

I can see that he's right but if he can gain a bit more altitude, perhaps the Huey could chew its way through the treetops without crashing. There's no other way out.

Hank comes on the net. "The gunship is in position and will be firing rockets into the tree line at those mother fuckers. He'll swing back around and spray the whole area with his miniguns."

Good to hear, however my main concern is to make it through the treetops that we're chopping our way into at the moment. The machine shudders but manages to stay airborne… and stay together. We're able to pick up enough lift as we gain speed dropping down the slope on the far side of the ridge.

"Good luck boys, and good flying. See you in Da Nang. 46 Whiskey off net."

I turn back in time to see smoke rising from the tree line where the NVA troops originally made their attack from. The Huey gunship makes one last pass, raking the whole area with his mini guns, then makes a sharp jerking movement as it gains altitude and follows us back towards Da Nang.

CHAPTER 14:

NVA SOLDIERS

CAPTAIN BAO AND SERGEANT CHANH ARE WATCHING FROM their position on the tree line as two helicopters approached the ridge where the battle was taking place. No air support visible at this time. One small observation aircraft circles at altitude beyond rifle range. The two choppers land quickly and the gunners on board fire blindly in their direction. Both NVA take cover behind a large tree where they can observe safely. Sgt. Chanh has given orders to his soldiers, before they have engaged the puppet troops, to pull back if an extraction by helicopter is taking place. No need to die if they are leaving in defeat. However, some of his men keep charging the helicopters and a few go down.

A white man is visible loading the troops onto the nearest chopper which eventually limps up and away from the battlefield. Suddenly a Huey gunship appears overhead firing rockets in their direction. Both commanders hit the ground as well as the troops out front who see what's happening. Sergeant Chanh raises his AK as the machine comes through on a low pass firing its machine guns in the direction of the troops left on the ground. He aims towards this flying monster as it speeds by and empties his clip. The chopper leaves the area. This time for good. Perhaps Sgt. Chanh's bullets have found their mark.

He walks out into the battle area to access the wounded and dead' Pvt. Cong approaches him.

"Sgt. Chanh, we have had one man in our platoon killed, Corporal Anh. There are others wounded however not so bad that they will have to be carried. The other platoons had more casualties but not so much more than us."

"That is a tragedy for the family of Corporal Anh," replies Chanh. "He came so close to surviving at least five years of fighting, Please have our men carry his body back to our base camp. I will gather together the rest and prepare for the journey with a sad heart."

Private Huu has tears in his eyes as he helps carry the wrapped body of the corporal who had been a good friend. Sergeant Chanh joins back up with Captain Bao as they make their way along the trail that leads toward their camp. They're walking along the trail, talking as they go.

"You were lucky Chanh. You were able to go back to your village and see your family and friends and the one you love. I have not been back home for five years. I worry that I might not ever make it back. Makes me nervous, not scared but nervous. Mostly for my wife and kids. The kids are almost grown up now and they will not recognize me. I hope my wife will know me. So many years apart, one cannot know those things."

"I'm sure that your family will not have forgotten you Captain, and I am sure that your wife is waiting. Be positive. And I know how lucky I was to be able to return. And for that I have you to be grateful. Thank you again Captain Bao."

CHAPTER 15:

DA NANG AIRFIELD

THE GUN SHIP PASSES US AS WE NEAR THE DA NANG AIR-
field. It doesn't look right but is able to land in one piece. Barns slides our
machine in right on its heels. There's a triage unit adjoining the helicopter
apron. Barns has radioed ahead for assistance and immediately after landing
attendants are waiting with stretchers alongside the ramp.

Omar is directing the offloading of troops, the wounded and the bodies. At this point I'm holding Banks up for he's passed out and has lost a lot
of blood.

"Hurry Omar, we have to lift Banks out of here and move him to triage
quicky or we might lose him. Let's move." I'm stressed and shaking.

"I be here" Omar replies. He's dragged a stretcher to the side of the
chopper and as easily as possible we lay Banks on it and trot immediately to
the triage building. I'm thinking it's too bad the 95th Evacuation Hospital
had been disbanded a couple of years earlier, for that was a first class and
complete medical facility.

At any rate Banks is left with the attending medics who get right on
him. After a quick check they indicate that he should make it.

"Bad day, my captain," says Omar, and I agree.

He leaves to check in with ARVN Marine headquarters to see how the men in total have made out. I return to the chopper to find Barns and offer some help. He's sitting with his feet on the skids looking exhausted.

"How you doing old man," I venture while walking towards him.

"I'm a whipped man and not afraid to admit it. You look so yourself. How's Banks?"

"They thought he'd make it. I left him at triage. We should drop back there before we leave."

"You know Ed, I've had it, and I've known that for some time. Just didn't want to admit it to myself. You know how long I've been involved over here. Five years…and what's there to show for it. The countries worse off and I'm worse off. Fuck it. It'll be over soon, and I'll move on. I can't be picking up these kids that are all shot up and dying and dead any longer. Doesn't matter to me if they're locals or Americans. It's over the top. I think I need Van Ly." That brings a smile to his face, and to me. And I was thinking, I need Lien.

"What the fuck are you doing here Winslow? I haven't seen you, or for that matter thought of you since the night in that shack in Tam Hiep, where officers were not allowed or for that matter any GI of rank or persuasion was allowed." It's Hank Sleet, the old warhorse himself who has walked over to the Huey to check in with us. He'd looked into the gunship that seemed to be limping home and found that it did take a hit from an AK round to a hydraulic line, but luckily made it back.

Barns looks up and thanks him for his help earlier in the day and I introduce them.

"Glad to meet you, Colonel. But I'm curious to know, why is a colonel out spotting for an ARVN operation in a Bird Dog"?

"Long story Major Barns. Let's meet up for a beer this evening and get with it. You know a good bar?"

I gave him directions to the Bamboo, and we agree to meet up with him there. This has to be an interesting story. Him flying out there today makes no sense.

"So Ed," says Barns, "How do you happen to know him?"

"We crossed paths on occasion back in '68, I think it was, mostly at the Bien Hoa Air Base. He had spent a year in Thailand at Udorn where he flew bombing runs up North to Hanoi with F-105s. His next tour was Air Force Liaison Officer with the 173rd Airborne that was headquartered in Bien Hoa , and where I was working on and off. Not to mention Tam Hiep, a little off limits village that we both favored, a peaceful oasis from the military world where we each had found female companionship. We were not bosom buddies by any means but were always friendly. I think he even was acquainted with Omar who was in Tam Hiep for the same reason as us. That's about it. I'm sure we'll hear more tonight. I'd like to think we could go over today's operation first, if that's what you'd call it. What a clusterfuck."

Barns has a few last minute checks to perform on his Huey before he looks in on Banks. I walk over to Marine headquarters to share my thoughts with General Luong. The days operation left a bad taste in my mouth. Not so much how it played out, but just why were we there at all. Our small cavalcade of Hueys was not going to drive the NVA from the A Shau. No chance of that. So why were we there?

"We were there to show the invading enemy from the North that they will not easily take over the South," General Luong replies in an angry tone, as if I were accusing him of causing the day's catastrophe "We were there because our soldiers need to feel that they can be effective against the enemy. How do we know that it will end this way? We cannot know. This be war...so be it."

I tell the general how sorry I am that he had lost so many men. It is not just the uneven battle after all. The helicopter with its crew and ten soldiers that had gone down was a double tragedy. And two machines were lost in the end. The ARVN are having trouble keeping helicopters in the air due to the lack of mechanics and spare parts that had plagued air operations since the Americans pulled out. The lack of serviceable aircraft can indeed be a double tragedy if it comes down to a final battle with not enough air support.

Eventually the evening finds the four of us, Barns, Hank, Omar and myself at the Bamboo ordering drinks from the intriguingly beautiful Van Ly along with my sweet Lien. The conversation has not yet moved to beautiful women…most pointedly to these beautiful women.

"I've had close calls," said Barns, "but I'd like to think that today was my last one. I was sure we'd go down while chopping through those treetops. I have no idea how that rotor held together. "

"Good that it did," is all I can add. "I certainly don't care to be with you the next time, Barns."

"No next time" Barns comes back with. "Maj. Jake Barns fini war."

"I've said that many times over the years" interjects Colonel Hank, "and we seem to be nearing the end of my third war. Who can know, my son?"

Hank will usually get into his flying in China or Korea by this time, however he too seems more interested in Van Ly. I'd previously let him know that Lien was with me. Not that he had any honor along those lines.

"She is beautiful. Reminds me of a girl I knew in Seoul many years ago'

And so it goes, the age-old stories of men at war in foreign lands where their main interest is always the women. I change the subject back to this war, so that Jake can keep his fantasies of Van Ly to himself.

" Yea, well I got shot down in China in my P-40" Hank is saying, "but luck was with me. My chute opened and I landed near the river that separated our forces from the Japs, so I swam to safety. Pretty simple at the time, however youth played the biggest part. At that age you're always sure you're not going to die, and able to escape any mess, somehow. Actually, I was more worried about being captured if I was able to land safely. I'd been hit while shooting up a wagon caravan of wounded Japs. Now mind you I didn't realize that until finishing up. However, you don't want'em to catch you after pulling one of those."

"Was that the first time you jumped with a chute," I ask him, letting the previous story go.

"Yup, but there was one more. With the 173rd Airborne on the only large-scale parachute jump of this war in the Iron Triangle. We didn't accomplish a hell of a lot, but the chute worked."

"Are you through now?" I asked him, "finished with war."

"For sure boys. I was out there today just for the hell of it. Indications were for no contact, or so General Luong told me. Officially I'm signed out. Retired. Just up here to check things out and say my goodbyes. General Luong is an old friend. No idea you'd be here Winslow? Not at all. Completely unexpected. Must admit though that I did have a good time flying above you fellas today. A little excitement never hurt anyone."

"Bull shit," said Barns. "One clean shot from an NVA AK and you could have bought the farm. No retirement for you Colonel Hank Sleet."

"Yes my boy, but they missed. I'm out of here in the morning for Cam Ranh Bay and a ride home. I know I'm finished with the wars forever this time. And good riddance."

"So where too? Weren't you from somewhere up in the Adirondacks?"

"Yea, up in the sticks. Bloomingdale. Think I'll move into Lake Placid. Got a friend there that runs the FBO at the airport who needs a charter pilot and flight instructor. I'll try that for a spell. Or I might get on with Fed Ex. You heard about them? They're just starting up, but the future looks good for the air freight business."

I was thinking he's lucky to be moving on from Vietnam and that I'm looking forward to the same. With Lien of course, who's getting tired of the war talk.

"If you come late to our house my Captain, please do not wake me."

I assure her that I'll be along in good time and that I certainly will not disturb her sleep. We still have to go over the days clusterfuck; which on the surface looks pretty simple. Our force landed to investigate an area and was surprised by a larger enemy unit. Maybe there isn't a lot more to say. We were lucky to get as many out as we did, including ourselves.

Omar has been quiet. I think he was intimidated by Hank. He thinks the only problem was lack of air support.

"Before when I with the Marines, last year or two for sure, we had air support very quickly when needed. Now it be gone. No Americans flying helicopter. That be alright, we have good pilots, but not enough mechanics or spare parts. Same for fighter aircraft. We be done."

He made some very good points that I agree with one hundred per cent. I'm sure Barns does also.

"Yea, I've been lucky in that regard. All three wars I've fought in were well supplied with parts and mechanics. However I do see your point Omar," Hank says.

Barns, who has been visiting with Van Ly puts in, "there is one problem here. We have been left in fighting positions with varying support and no real mission…except to be here."

"Hang in there," It's Hank again. "You'll be ok. I've got to be on my way. Good to know you Maj. Barns and Sgt. Omar. And so pleasant to meet up with you so unexpectedly Captain Winslow. If you end up back in Port Kent, even if only for a visit, look me up. Just call the FBO in Lake Placid. So long now… and stay safe. Good by Van Ly, you beautiful thing you.".

And with that the old warrior, and hound dog, leaves us. No way of telling if I'll ever see him again.

"What's up for you tomorrow Omar," I ask him.

"You know Captain, I have not seen my wife and kids for months. They live in Saigon as you know. Tomorrow General Luong said that he would find me a ride down so that I could visit them for few days. After that, I be back. I never leave you, my Captain."

Omar is a good guy, and they are scarce and getting scarcer. He leaves and I remain on the stool alongside Jake Barns while he's getting nowhere with Van Ly.

" I like you very much Major Barns. My reservations have nothing to do with you personally. It has to do with my family and others that I know who I am friends with. I cannot discuss much of that with you. Maybe later when we see what happens here. I have to go to Hue tomorrow to see my family and some other people. I will talk more with you when I return."

"Good night Van Ly. See you whenever." And with that farewell Barns and I leave the Bamboo, me for Lien's place and he back to his pad at the air base. Tomorrow will be another day.

I was in the mess hall having coffee the next morning mulling over the past day's operations, one more time, when Art Everest drops in.

"Mind if I join you," he directs at me.

"Love to have you, Arthur. You can pep me up."

He comes over with coffee and a plate of eggs and sausage. Must be the mess had a good shipment. They'd had no breakfast meats for over a week. And SEALS need their protein.

"I heard it was a bit of a push for you yesterday, wasn't it Ed?"

"Push is hardly the word for it. If those two choppers hadn't made it back in, we'd have all died. Much to close for me this late in the game."

"If I'd been in on the planning it wouldn't have happened. My team has penetrated that whole area recently. It's somewhat infested with NVA and there's no use risking anyone's life poking around there. Period. We Seals do have a mission, and we fulfill it."

"I was only there because I speak Vietnamese and would be able to help if any air support was called in. Omar, their regular interpreter was along also however at times it's necessary to have some extra help getting the message from the field to air support headquarters. We're short of air now. Too many

THE DISILLUSIONED

birds, choppers and fighters, are DXed for parts and maintenance. That's not going to change any time soon."

"It's all more of the same. Don't let it fuck up your head. Hell, I'm ready to head back to Little Creek and take it easy for a while. Check in with the wife and kids. Get my drift?"

I have to laugh. I know he is extremely attached to his wife and kids. In spite of the Seal bravado.

"I'll tell you though, Ed. I was part of a team that assassinated for the Phoenix Program, partially in this area, but mostly west of Hue, back in '72. We were having trouble with lack of artillery even back then. Most of the time it didn't matter a hell of a lot. You don't need that kind of support when your mission is to enter a VC hooch and cut throats. Pretty simple."

"You can have it," I said. "Do you ever think that's why we're losing."

"Sure, but that's the job we're trained for. Take orders, ID the 'bad guy'… and terminate."

Too much for me. I make my goodbyes and leave to find Lien and take her out for pho.

CHAPTER 16:

NVA BASE CAMP

IT HAD BEEN A FEW DAYS SINCE SGT. CHANH AND HIS PLA-
toon returned from the battle with the puppet troops. Their losses had
been few however their morale had suffered. Captain Bao and Chanh are
discussing just that, as they sit outside their command bunker enjoying an
early morning tea. The camp is quiet. A number of the men have been out
on night patrols or on perimeter guard and are resting, having sacked out in
hammocks strung among the trees.

"I think our soldiers will pick up the will to fight when we can begin
our Spring offensive which could lead to a final victory. I understand them.
I cannot go on much longer myself. I need to go home." said Capt. Bao.

"We have all worked hard for many years Captain, but this war will end
soon. I'm with you. I believe even the new troops under our command feel
the same. It doesn't take years to become disillusioned. There are times when
months or weeks or even days will do the trick. The masters who direct this
war back in Hanoi are sometimes very distant from the reality here in the
field. Most of them. I know a few of the old warriors are listened to, however

much of the new leadership has never been under the guns and bombs down the trail as we have. There is much they don't know."

"You're right Sgt. Chanh," said Captain Bao. "But you can cheer up for this afternoon, maybe later in the afternoon, we will have a show. One of the entertainment troops has arrived overnight and is now resting. They will be performing before the evening meal."

"That will be a good thing captain. It will lift the men's spirits. I think I will now take a rest till the men come around. I'm tired too, very tired."

The camp was coming alive. Some of the men were washing in a nearby creek. Some were having tea and wishing it were a cold beer. Maybe even rice wine would do. However, the main event was the show that was happening shortly. Chanh was talking with two of the show girls. It was Ca and Hue, the two girls he'd met on his trek home weeks earlier.

"It is so good to see you both again," said Chanh. "I'd thought never again as I headed north with the wounded on my way back home."

"We are as surprised as you," said Ca. "Hue and I thought the same. We never see you again."

"So we are all very lucky. And now we can watch your troupe entertain us all. My men will be so excited. They have not seen many women down here. We are off the main trail enough so that the repair gangs don't come this way often. But you are here. All you beautiful girls."

With that Ca and Hue smiled but took their leave to prepare with the rest of the troupe for the nights event. Private Huu approached Chanh and inquired about the girls. He'd not been aware that there was going to be real show.

"Private Huu," said Chanh, "you will see a performance like you have never experienced. I know these girls."

He proceeded to tell Huu of his meeting up with this troupe on his trip home and how he knew the main singer Ca. Private Huu was worked up by this and returned to his bunker to spread the word to his mates.

The show was a smash hit. The setting, an open bed of a Russian truck that was parked under a canopy of green. Trees that had grown back or survived the massive spraying that had occurred here over the years. There was a slight breeze that kept the men cool as Ca sang songs of young love and Vietnamese patriotism. Some of the older men like Captain Bao were seen crying, drying their tears. When she finished a quiet calm came over the camp. The men retreated into the privacy of their own minds.

The next morning a messenger from Base 611 rode into camp on a motorbike. Chanh watched as he went over to company headquarters thinking something must be up. After all they had radio contact throughout their theatre. It turned out to not be specific, there was nothing definite however the men must be prepared to move at a moment's notice and must have all of their equipment and supplies and armaments in top shape. Something was in the air.

CHAPTER 17:

BACK IN DA NANG

I'M SPENDING THE NIGHT TUCKED IN WITH LIEN INSIDE
our place on Tran Phu Street, downtown Da Nang. We cling to each other
after a sweet night of lovemaking, talking and planning for our future, whatever the hell that might be…. but we are hopeful.

It's the next morning and I'm beginning the long walk to the Air Base for a
talk with Jake Barns and Colonel Luong. As I reach the main drag that leads
toward the air base, I turn left, then left again at the river. I've been thinking
that Wales Signor at the consulate might have more updated information
that could prove helpful later in the morning. Wales is up and getting busy.
He asks me to check back in a couple of days, and he'll have more data. He's
expecting something important.

Heading south along the river leads me past the Bamboo. Somehow it
is always there. I notice Van Ly bustling around inside and there are no customers, so I figure to stop in for a coffee and see what's going on. She's been
away for a few days on a trip to Hue, supposedly to visit relatives.

I'm still curious about Van Ly. Regardless, I walk in, say hi and order a café de lait, without the sugar. This is impossible but I always try. I wasn't always aware that condensed milk was sweet.

"Never happen GI," said Van Ly. "In Viet Nam coffee always be sweet. We no make American coffee here." And she smiled.

"OK Van Ly, could you please make me a sweet coffee and I will make that do."

Another girl came in that I hadn't seen before. A quite beautiful, short and sexy young girl. Many before me have always sworn, that that's the real reason we have remained in Viet Nam for so many years.

Van Ly walks over with the coffee and introduces us. "Khanh, this is captain Edward Winslow who is a good friend, and an even better customer of the Bamboo. He is in love with Lien, so you cannot have."

Khanh turns to me, extends her hand and says, "glad to meet you captain. I work here sometimes, sometimes not, it depends."

So, two pretty girls for company at the present, and I've just spent the night with the one I love, and I'm thinking that Barns and the General can wait.

"How about you Khanh, where you from?"

"From Hue, same same Van Ly. But I like Da Nang."

About then a couple of ARVN troops came in for pho, so Khanh leaves to take care of them, and I began again with Van Ly. And as usual she is not that forthcoming.

"What does your family do in Hue?" I ask. "Must be a tough place to make a living."

"My mother runs a shop that sells everything Vietnamese, and other things too. My father is lame and cannot do much. He was badly wounded early in the war. For you I will tell… he was VC. No need to tell other American this."

"Hey, don't worry Van Ly, I understand. Who knows in a country where there is a civil war, which side to fight for? Maybe the one that make it best for you to survive?"

"No, that not be it. He fight for his country. Not for the Americans. No need to tell other American this either. Like I say to you before. I have family on the other side. Cousins. They never give up, and are positive now. They think soon."

This information did not shock me, but I was surprised that she was so open. I also wonder what was meant by 'soon'. On my first tour a number of years ago I was an infantry officer with the 25th Infantry in Cu Chi. Everyone knew about the tunnel system that crisscrossed that whole area. Even all the way to Saigon. The company I was with ran operations normally between Cu Chi and the Cambodian border and was not so involved with the tunnels. But they did go to the border there. This was where I began to teach myself Vietnamese, obviously with their help.

On these ops along the border, we'd at times pick up prisoners. Sometimes troops from the fighting and other times civilians that looked to be with the other side. I never liked depending on the interpreters that were with the ARVN, which was all we had for communication with them. Or even with the locals or other ARVN troops that sometimes accompanied us on our field operations. If the interpreters are from the home front, you're never sure if what you're hearing is correct. Let's face it, everyone's got their own agenda. The same goes for every political position. Furthermore, the ARVN did the torturing for information. Most Americans were too squeamish and just watched. I like to verify what is said. At any rate I did learn passable Vietnamese and have retained it to this day.

But it's not needed with Van Ly. She could be translating English to Vietnamese for the VC for all I know. There was no doubt that the girls who work in nearly all of the headquarter offices are in the know. As many before me have noticed, the GI girlfriends usually know their orders before they do. More customers are dropping in so I bid Van Ly farewell and ask that we can catch up later on.

"That be ok," she replied." Be sure you say goodbye to Khanh. She will like that."

I follow through with her command and head for the air base. After a good walk, eggs and bacon and toast and whatever else they have at the base mess hall will be just fine, will be delicious. The heat is picking up as the sun climbs in the sky. Looks to be a clear day with few clouds. I'm beginning to notice on my walk that there are next to no troops on the streets, neither US nor ARVN. It looks odd. It seems odd. That's why I need to have a good talk with Barns and the General too, if he is still available. There's always the chance he's had recent contact with his friend Polger, the CIA man from the Embassy. When I finally arrive at the mess hall Barns is waiting.

"Where the hell have you been," he declares. "You have any idea how long I've been waiting for you?"

"Come on Jake, I know you like to sleep in. Usually it's me who's kept waiting. Sorry for that. I checked in at the consulate to see Wales Signor first, then stopped at the Bamboo. You know how it is. By the way, do you know Khanh, the new girl from the bar, new for me at least."

"Hell no, what's she looks like?" I fill him on the girls, then on to the General who he mentions has come and gone.

He's heard from Polgar, the CIA chief though, and did fill me in… to the extent you'd expect. You ever notice that everyone over here has a secret or keeps a secret or at least lets you think that's the case.

"You know that Polgar is Hungarian" he begins, "and that there are Hungarian and Polish representatives on the ICCS. He was made a citizen before being drafted in WW2, then went to the OSS and eventually to the CIA. He's been station chief here for a few years, I don't recall how many. At any rate he's been working with the Polish and Hungarian reps from that commission to try and work out something with Russia who supposedly can influence the North Vietnamese towards some kind of political settlement before they over run us."

"Sounds like bull shit to me," I tell him. "Why would they make a deal at this point?"

Barns agrees with me on this issue. Otherwise, General Luong had nothing specific in the way of news. His orders were to 'hold and secure'.

"Have you seen Everest or Peters lately? I ask him. "They may have something."

"Well, what do you think? They always assume they're ahead of everyone else when it comes to 'intelligence'. Oh, hell, let's get some eggs and sausage and we'll be good till happy hour. I need to check out the new bar maid. Can't seem to get anywhere with Van Ly. Too reserved...and secretive "

"Well Jake my boy, you know how it is. She has people on 'the other side'. That's a good reason to hold your cards close."

CHAPTER 18:

US CONSULATE, DANANG

I WAS WALKING WITH BARNS AND OMAR ALONG THE RIVER towards the Bamboo. Since it was a bit early for Happy Hour we decide to check in at the consulate and see if anything new had happened. Omar has concerns since he still hasn't seen his family in Saigon, and he obviously does not want to be stranded up here when or if things come to a head. We walk by a youngish boy who is standing by the river watching us pass.

He shouts "Fuck you Americans. You go home now."

Omar wants to give him a slap, but I persuade him to ignore the kid. What does it matter? However, it is disconcerting. Da Nang has always been a friendly town overall. Two other pedestrians give us the evil eye as they walk by.

"They're afraid," I think, "it's fear of the unknown. And who else would they blame? Look around the country and it's easy to see why. Have a talk with Emerson Fitz. I hate to sound like an earthy GI private, but we've been fucking over these people for ten years, and how's it look? That's your answer."

Omar remains silent but cracks a smile as we continue toward the consulate. I know he has something to say and finally ask him what he's thinking.

"Many of my people are angry because they cannot now make much money off you Americans. Too many go home, and your government has very little resupply now. It be hard living for Da Nang people who before make money off GI. Maybe work for American government in headquarters or for constructing bases. It be serious. They must eat and feed family. At same time it be all about dollars. We love money."

I think, well yes but it does take dollars to survive and it's no joke to be without. Omar's perspective can sometimes be unknown. We meet Wales as he leaves the front door of the consulate. He suggests that we walk out on the pier across the street that protrudes some ways into the river, a pier that was more ceremonial than commercial. There are benches along the edge, and we all take a seat and watch the shipping for a spell, saying nothing.

Finally, I ask him if he has any news of importance "You must be in the loop Wales, what have you heard?"

"Actually, I had a long talk with the Embassy in Saigon this morning," he reveals. The word from Graham Martin, US Ambassador to this country, is that there remains plenty of time. South Vietnam is not going to fall. He believes Big Minh will replace Thieu and some sort of accommodation with the North will be made."

"Personally, I would view that scenario as being very unlikely, but what do I know?"

"You don't know nothing GI" is Wales's comeback wisecrack.

"But to be serious" he continues, "I do think that Martin is somewhat removed from reality. He has just returned from the States and hasn't been well. He isn't now. And there's another thing, back in the States they still do not think that a collapse here is eminent. They believe that the CIA and the DOA on this side are overstating the case. So, we'll see. "

After all that, we inform Signor that it's off to the Bamboo for happy hour. Enough for now, and thanks. He indicates that he'll stop in later if things work out. This means that there is a consulate cocktail party to attend to first. Barns is anxious to meet Khanh, 'just for the hell of it' he said, and why not. I was hoping to meet up with Everest or Leonard for a change in conversation. Omar is being quiet...too quiet for a guy who will never stop talking.

It turns out the only white man in the bar is Emerson Fitz...in a subdued, smoldering mood.

"Do you guys realize that you've burned, bombed, sprayed or plowed under nearly the surface of this country, less the cities? Do you?"

I begin thinking that here we go again. All that he says is true, but why can't he just let it go? It's too late now. We can't undo it.

"Look it Fitz," interjects Barns. "I came here to be introduced to a girl, Khanh I believe her name is, and to escape from the world out there. Please...for now."

Barns goes over and introduces himself to Khanh, at the same time ordering a round from Van Ly who sets us all up. Omar remains quiet. I hoped that we'd see Lien but not yet. Must be she's working the late shift. I never know. Even to me her life is private.

"You know what set me off Winslow? As I was leaving the office there was an old clip on the TV of Morley Shafer's piece on the burning of the hooches in Cam Ne which must have been filmed ten years ago. I was up in Tra My recently and many of the houses that were burned or bombed off up there are still not rebuilt. Pissed off isn't the word for it. Maybe righteous anger. Do you guys realize that you've burned off 90 percent of the houses in the countryside of Viet Nam by now. Think that's enough?"

"Look it Fitz, I get it, but it's a done deed. None of us can do anything about that. All I can say is that it's unlikely any more will be torched. Maybe there'll be some kind of reconstruction program by the US when this is all over."

"I wouldn't count on it" he angrily replies. "Most Americans are sour on this scene. They just want to forget it, and it's so far away they'll be able to."

Wouldn't we all like to forget it I'm thinking. The war, that is. I love everything else here. Fitz turns silent while he drinks his beer. Barns come over, apparently without much luck with Khanh.

"Must be losing my touch." he mumbles. "Must be getting old."

I can see Van Ly talking with Khanh at the end of the bar and am thinking that they both likely have very different agendas, with different people. Not with Barns or anyone else among the American crowd. We're extras in this production. And I'm the lucky one, I have Lien. Fitz finishes his beer and leaves without a word. No telling what he's thinking. Then I notice Omar at the other end talking with Van Ly. I head down there.

"You two talking old times, or relatives?" Omar turns my way looking confused. Van Ly smiles and begins mixing a whiskey coke. She knows me.

"We just talk, my captain. Nothing more," Omar quietly says.

It's becoming difficult because I am in no way spying on my friends. I'm curious to see where all the pieces fit. And how the people fit into them. Van Ly can be distant, but Omar wants to talk.

"What do you mean Captain Winslow? Van Ly and I are of our country. She has family on both sides. Cousins fight for each army. Very bad. I have uncle who is colonel in NVA. I am ARVN and work for the Americans, for you. What can I say? Have another beer and say fuck it. In the end we all be losers, even you."

There is no way I can argue with that. But still, we aren't there yet. Furthermore, my hope is to escape to the ends of the earth, to Australia with Lien.

"Have you guys heard the news?" It's Art Everest who has just walked in with Len Peters. "Thieu has ordered his army from the Central Highlands. Ban Me Thuot is lost, apparently without a fight. It's the beginning of the end boys. Mark my words."

"We had word earlier from sources that this was coming but it was not believable. Why? What is the reason for this absolute capitulation of one of the most strategic parts of the country? It'll be cut in half," exclaims Peters "and there'll be no taking it back."

This bit of news takes the whole bar by surprise. But perhaps not Van Ly who has no reaction nor does Omar, which I think odd, so I press him on it.

"I hear same thing but wait to say anything. Never know," he replies.

Barns, Everest and Peters end up having their own conversation on the pros and cons of this military maneuver. I noticed that Van Ly is ignoring the whole thing, keeping busy behind the bar so I lean over to have a few words in private.

"Van Ly, news to you? You don't seem surprised."

"Never happen GI. I never surprised. I know things. This be news to me when I go to Hue few days ago, but not news tonight."

I'm beginning to remember what the girls would tell us in Tam Hiep so many years ago…. in this same war. They would know our orders before we did. For many reasons. Van Ly's explanation is along the same lines…and she has friends on 'the other side'.

"It be very simple my Captain. In Hue many people have connections with both sides. Same here with me. We be one people. I see my girlfriend in Hue. She love my cousin who fight with the Liberation Front. I do not say VC. That be American. Many who work for the Americans in Saigon are with the National Liberation Front. The tunnels in Cu Chi reach almost to Saigon boundary. Information can pass very easy. So, we know things. And I once heard you talk that the Vietnamese Grape Vine be very fast means of communication. That be true. We know, and for people like me it be about survival. We just want it to end. For me, I can live with either side. Just to end."

I think, why dig any farther. I'll leave that to Peters who is the 'military intelligence' guy. She has laid it out clearly enough for me.

"So, Leonard," I begin, "where did you acquire your information on this matter?"

"From Arthur here, he's in the know from the jungle," and he breaks into a smile which is rare for him when the speaks thus.

Arthur throws down his third straight Wild Turkey and began his discourse.

'You've got to get out in the field…into the hooches …underneath the undergrowth…beneath the streams. That's what we Seal's do and we've a handle on this. We're in the know. Give me a couple more teams and I'll hold off the whole fucking NVA in the A Shau. No problem. Another Turkey please Van Ly."

Then he drifts off into a conversation with her. Omar cocks his eye and looks at me as he hears that comment. He comes over and says quietly.

"Number ten fucking thou bull shit, this guy say. NVA kick his ass." He laughs a small laugh, "like I say before, my uncle be Colonel in NVA. No way man."

I certainly do not want to enter into a conversation with either the Seal or the Intel officer with Omar's comment. They'd be calling him a spy.…and who knows? Actually, Arthur does not take himself at all seriously. He's just blowing off steam. He comes over with an offer of a decidedly different kind.

"When we're back in the world Ed, I'd like to meet you up in Port Kent where we could relive these few days of our youth, whenever I have an opportunity to visit Lake Champlain. Doesn't your relative have a large house up there. Seems to me you mentioned that once."

"I did and he does. That would be my Watson relative who still lives in the house his ancestor built in the early 1800s. My Uncle Charles is a bachelor, consequently there would be no shortage of space."

"I'll try to work that out Arthur, if I'm not in Australia with Lien. That's my first choice…by a very long mile."

"You can't sell out your military buddies for a woman, Winslow, it's against the rules."

"Not my rule" I reply, and I'm not on the verge of drunkenness. "I'll sell out everything for her and I mean everything if I have to."

"Listen," came in Leonard Peters who normally avoided these issues. "There's no need for you to travel to some hick town like Port Kent to be on historic waters. My mother has a place on Buzzards Bay with ten bedrooms that has plenty of vacancies year-round. Skip the winter though. Any time else… if we make it out of here. Just let me know. There's a couple of boats there too so we'd be able to sail anywhere on the Cape you'd like."

A glance towards the rear by the river reveals Barns and Khanh playing pool. He must be getting somewhere.

About then I see Lien walk in, so I leave these birds to dream and talk among themselves. My plans will be made with the girl I love. Her first words do not differ from the previous conversations.

"Did you hear that President Thieu has ordered the army from Ban Me Thuot. This is not good. I am worried my captain."

I tell her to never worry. I will be going to Saigon shortly and will clarify things with my friend John Sanderson, the Aussie soldier who has good connections with the Australian Embassy. The place thinned out not so long after Lien arrives, so she is able close early. Barns disappears with Khanh which is hard to believe, but who can know. Before we leave, I tell Omar to meet me at the Consulate in the morning at 8:00 and we'll try to extract something permanent that would allow him transport to Saigon when necessary.

Lien and I stretch out in bed for a long time talking amidst periods or silence and love making till late into the night without arriving at any sure thing solution.

Omar meets me at the consulate next morning earlier than I'd requested so we have coffee on the street with Quan who is upbeat, regardless. He's survived it all.

"This be serious for me my Captain. For me I think I fight for freedom. When the other side looks at me, they see a traitor. I must be gone if they win."

A crowd is building along the consulate entrance, and it looks as if we'll have a difficult time entering. We walk over and Omar takes care of things. His command of authoritative Vietnamese does the trick, and an opening is made for us.

We enter into more chaos than we've seen outside. I tell Omar that I'd not expected this because such a rush didn't seem eminent.

"Not for you, but for them…and for myself. We be in big hurry. I see General Luong earlier this morning. He say Ban Me Thuot is captured and the NVA are beginning a drive to cut off Hue from the road south. That be only 50K north of here. They do same, same from Highlands toward Chu Lai 70k south. Da Nang will be an island. Maybe like pirate." Omar never completely abandoned his sense of humor. I assure him that arrangements will somehow be made in his favor. Wales promises a letter that would authorize transport for Omar and his family on any conveyance available when it becomes necessary.

CHAPTER 19:

_____

TU DO ST. SAIGON

I MAKE THE MORNING MILK RUN TO SAIGON ON A C-133 that normally flies from that normally flies from the States to Vietnam loaded with supplies, but today is filling in for a lowly C-47 that's broken down.

After landing and clearing the airport and catching a ride to the Post Office in Saigon, I walk down Tu Do St. to the Continental Hotel. It's obvious that the polish is wearing off the 'Paris of the Orient', but the streets are bustling as usual with traffic of every kind.

Jeeps, Duce and a Halfs, Five quarters and vehicles from both armies rule among a sea of Renault taxi cabs, Lambrettas, Motorbikes, Cyclos, bicycles, even the occasional horse drawn cart. Things looked normal with no hint of an impending collapse. Actually, considering how much has gone down in this city over the last thirty years, the population expects anything, and nothing.

I walk on by the Continental and stop in front of the Opera House which is faced by that ugly statue of an ARVN soldier, then stop and looked back up Tu Do wondering if I should go back to Girval or the Continental Shelf or continue to the Caravelle and see if anyone I know is about. Before making my decision, out from the Shelf walks John Sanderson, the very friend that I need to have a conversation with, possibly the most important conversation I will ever have. Sandy notices me and walks across the street.

"Well fuck me dead," Sandy exclaims, "Didn't expect to see you down here in this town Captain, with all the excitement going on up your way."

"How you doing Sandy? You're just the guy I'm looking for. How about stopping at the Kangaroo for a brew and a talk?"

"Sure thing Captain. Let' go."

The Kangaroo bar is just a block past the Air France office which is on the bottom floor of the Caravelle Hotel. It's the headquarters bar for the Aussie Embassy that's located in that hotel. Sandy, first in Vietnam as a soldier with the Australian Army, has moved up to a security position at the Embassy. Says he'd like to stay in Vietnam forever. I think he's on his second, unofficial Vietnamese wife, not to mention the girlfriends.

The Kangaroo isn't much different than in earlier years, maybe in need of a coat of paint but Tot is still running the joint. After greetings we sit down at the bar for a cold one. She always has Heinekens on ice.

I fill Sandy in on whatever I know on the happenings in Da Nang and Hue, then pump him for any information he's come across that could be useful.

"I don't have much else to offer," he replies. "You're ahead of me."

"How's your work going in the Embassy?"

"Fucking great mate. Besides security, lately I've been busy helping out issuing visas, mostly to local girls that have had attachments with soldiers back when they were involved in the fighting. You know most of them left by early '73. Of course, there's a lot of stragglers with all kinds of connections, so a lot to sort out."

"Well Sandy, when you're at it how about sorting it out with a visa for me and my girl Lien? Think you can pull it off?"

"You know this country. Anything's possible…except winning this fucking war. When it falls in, the word is I might end up at the Embassy when they move it to Hanoi. That ought to be a gas. But yes, I sure as hell can take care of your visas. Get your passports to me asap, but it might take a few days. Maybe not. We'll see."

"Good man Sandy, good man. Let me buy another beer."

It's a hot, like all days here. He motions to Tot, and she sends over one of the girls. Khanh is her name, another one… and Sandy introduces us. I have a feeling she might be more than a bar maid to him.

"Khanh, a tea for you too," I think to say.

She brings the Heinekens and joins us.

"I like to go to Australia too," she begins. "Is that not right Sandy?"

"Oh isn't she a sweet Sheila," he replies, "and if I do get sent to Hanoi she can stay at the farm outside of Sydney my folks still run. Plenty of room. Who knows?"

That kind of banter went on for a time until I ask him if there has ever been word of what happened to Flynn and Stone who disappeared in Cambodia in 1970. They'd covered the Nixon sponsored invasion and apparently been captured, and not heard from again to my knowledge. I'd met them both years back in the sixties. They lived on Tu Do street in the building just across from the Kangaroo alley out front. And Flynn being the son of Erroll was famous in his own right without being such an accomplished war photographer. Stone was a postman's son from central Vermont, across Lake Champlain from my uncle's place in Port Kent.

"Not a word, and I've read that Flynn's mother has spent a fortune looking for him. Their friend and fellow photographer Tim Page has stopped in over the years and has tried different approaches also, but to no avail. Don't think much information will be available until the war's over, and who knows what the hell's going to happen then."

"One more beer Khanh and I have to hit the road…if you please."

"Don't' rush off mate. We've a long night head of us in this old town."

"Can't do it this time Sandy. Too much going on. A friend flying an Air America Volpar is leaving for Da Nang in an hour and a half, so I've got to drink up and get moving."

"Good enough Captain. Just get those passports to me and you'll have your visas."

I assure him that I'll either be back soon with them or would send they down another way.

The Air America flight to Da Nang is on schedule and I make it back in the Bamboo in time for a nightcap with Lien and Van Ly who are about to shut the joint down for the night. I fill in Lien quickly on my meeting with Sandy. Van Ly serves me a glass of Courvoisier, knowing my preference at this hour.

"Thank you, Van Ly…thanks loads. It's been a busy day."

She looks worried so I made inquiries.

"I am scared about what will happen Captain Ed. I never say before but cousins in Tra My who are with what you call the VC, also scared. They be like me. They want no more war. They think the army from the North is ready to take over and move towards Da Nang. They say that the ARVN who were stationed in Tra My have all disappeared. Their leaders go first so they don't know. Change out of uniform and try to get home. Many are from that area. Some are from Saigon and just hide. They scared."

I try to explain that no one knows what will happen. Too many variables. I had thought that Van Ly would have been concerned first about her family in Hue after hearing about the situation up there from Wales.

"What about Hue, Van Ly?"

She starts crying, saying through her tears "I don't know. How can I? Last I hear many, many people will come this way if northern army enters the city."

Omar comes in for a last beer. He's never up this late, so there must be a reason. I ask him what's going on.

"Never know my Captain. General Luong very quiet. I talk with your friends Everest and Peterson early tonight at mess hall. They don't say much. Say don't know. I have girl friend whose family is from the village of Ky La by Marble Mountain. Even there, VC come every night. They talk. Soon I must get to Saigon."

I had to lighten the conversation up. "What about the girlfriend Omar? You have wife and kids in Saigon, and you're very worried about them and need to return to your family."

"That all be true Captain Ed, but wife be there, and I be here. So what can I do?"

I have no answer for that. Omar leaves while Lien and I return to our pad to be by ourselves where the closeness of our bodies wipes out the slowly encroaching world.

CHAPTER 20:

NVA IN

THE JUNGLE

A COLUMN OF RAGGED, WALKING WOUNDED NVA SOLDIERS
wind down a shattered jungle trail. Pvt. Huu and Sgt. Chanh are among the
column and are helping the walking wounded to stay on their feet and keep
moving. Along with the wounded in that column are two ARVN prisoners.
They are young and green. Their rank is private. Sgt. Chanh had taken his
platoon on a two-day exploratory mission south and east of the southern
end of the A Shau. Their orders were not to engage the enemy, just learn and
understand the terrain in the direction of Da Nang. It may well be that the
ARVN unit was under similar orders. At any rate they encountered each
other, and a furious battle ensued. No reserves were called in by either side
and air and artillery were absent from the ARVN. The NVA unit had lost
twelve men, with many seriously wounded. These were bringing up the rear
on stretchers born by their fellow soldiers.

"We should be back at our base in a couple of more hours Pvt. Huu. We all are dead tired however we must interrogate these two puppet soldiers when we arrive, as well as tend to the dead and wounded."

"Yes Sgt Chanh, we will. You know we won that battle even considering our losses, but Sgt Chanh, I don't feel we won. For me, the way I think, we cannot win. I have been fighting with you and this unit long enough for me to know how it ends. Not well. It's not win or lose, it is to live…and go home. My history with the army is very short, compared to yours of nearly ten years."

"Listen Pvt. Huu. First of all, you must keep that kind of opinion to yourself. It could bring much trouble on you if the cadre enforcers get wind of it. Be careful. I think it could end soon for all of us. The real mission is to stay alive until that happens. About our prisoners, we will all take a rest, as will they when we arrive. We are too tired for anything more."

Later in the evening after Chanh and his men handed off the wounded and the dead to the appropriate cadre and had slept for some hours, Chanh was thinking about his prisoners. It would be interesting to see how they thought, what they thought. He had no idea. The prisoners too had eaten and slept. It was time to interrogate them.

"What are your names?"

"I am Duc," said the larger one. "My friend is Dung."

"How long have you been in the puppet army?"

"Only for a year. We were friends before they picked us off the streets of Saigon and have been able to stay together so far. It is the only good thing about the whole year."

"What about you Dung? You look skinny. Do they feed you?"

"Not so good but we live," he answered haltingly.

It turned out that both of these soldiers, before being impressed into military service, had been 'Saigon Cowboys'. This was the preferred term for petty criminals and delinquents that lived off the streets of Saigon from their motorbikes, pillaging as they cruised past unsuspecting victims. With most of the Americans gone they had been having a tough time 'making a living' before becoming soldiers in the ARVN. Sargent Chanh had never heard that term and probed further.

"I know cowboys from stories of other soldiers who were more fortunate than I was when they were young and were able to see movies in Hanoi. They shoot guns and farm cows. Did you guys have guns on the streets of Saigon?"

"No, not at all" replied Duc. "We would ride around and steal watches from the GIs, Just grab and pull off the wrist as we rode by. It was fun and easy. They would get so angry and shout at us and say that they would kill all fucking gooks. We liked getting them. Sometimes steal even more."

Chanh was curious about how living was in the South. Soldiers from the north had been told they would be rescuing their fellow Vietnamese from an oppressive government that was controlled by the Americans and had enslaved the common man.

"There are many troubles in the South" interjected Dung, "but much more outside Saigon and the other larger cities. On the edge of the cities, where people from the countryside have moved to escape the bombing and other war violence, people are very poor. Many in the cities have money from the Americans who spend many dollars in Viet Nam."

"So you guys lived by stealing. Maybe it is a good thing you are in the army. You can learn some good things. Even in the ARVN."

Duc and Dung were beginning to think that they had said enough. Maybe too much.

"That doesn't matter now. We are in the army, and we want the war to end. That be it. Except maybe what you are going to be doing with us. Please don't shoot us. We are good people."

Chanh broke into a slight smile at that remark.

"We do not shoot our fellow Vietnamese. We do not shoot American POWs either. We obey the Geneva Conventions regarding that issue. Now all prisoners are sent north on the Trung Son Trail which provides very fast transport. I myself have traveled it recently to visit my home. You will be treated well. There are prisoner of war camps for you people. When the war ends you will be sent home. Don't worry about that. And never fear, it will be us that wins the war."

Huu has been listening but staying out of the conversation. It was all so strange for a soldier who had grown up in the northern countryside.

"Sgt. Chanh, I hope that we will be able to be part of the conquering army that continues south to Saigon. I want to see for myself what these guys are talking about."

Chanh assured him that that would more than likely be the scenario. The alternative was to be among the dead and wounded which he at this time would not mention. Hope was what kept his company going. He ordered Huu to take charge of these two prisoners for the night. They were to be sent to a holding compound at Base 611 in the morning.

Chanh left for the fire and a tea before checking the perimeter prior to sacking out. Captain Bao joined him.

"Those prisoners taken care of for the night, Sgt. Chanh?"

"They are in the charge of Private Huu. All is well."

Both men sat around the fire for a time, enjoying the heat as well as the tea. It could be chilly in these parts this time of year. Eventually they began discussing the possibility of eminent troop movement towards Da Nang, assumed to be their immediate destination when word is given to move forward. The trek through the mountains would not be that easy for their battalion. The American built roadway had deteriorated over time and been much overtaken by new growth. It hadn't been heavily traveled since the great battles of the Tet of 1968 when the First Air Cavalry Division swept through on Operation Delaware. The A Shau Valley had been under the control of the NVA since the Special Forces Camp at the southern end had been taken over in 1966. The only challenge to that had been the 1st Cav operation in 1968 and shortly thereafter the road had again fallen into the hands of the NVA.

"We have to cross the mountains between us and Da Nang. They are only a thousand meters high but are very steep, and the roads have been badly damaged by the weather with little repair over the years."

"I'm not looking forward to it in some ways " said Chanh, "but it is necessary. Then home for me, forever."

"I have no argument with that outlook Sgt. Chanh. I will be at your side."

CHAPTER 21:

US CONSULATE,

DA NANG

"YOU GUYS BETTER GET YOUR ACT TOGETHER," SAID Emerson Fitz. "The end is coming."

Chi fixed us coffee and we're sitting out in front of his office watching the morning push along the river. For myself the beautiful, quiet beginning to the day signified nothing in the way of 'the end'... and I tell him so. He laughs like hell.

"Listen Ed, I've been here for so many years I can smell the future and by that I mean the US presence is rapidly coming to an end. Mine too... however I am not leaving till they throw me out. Not Chi though. She has to leave for the States, sooner than later."

"Are you two married?" I asked him. He's so secretive about his private life.

"Maybe...maybe not." And that's that.

"I assume you've obtained a visa for her, and a ticket out. Don't wait."

"You think I don't know that? Both are taken care of. She's to leave next week. Air Vietnam to Saigon, then Hong Kong. She has friends there and will stay on for a bit to see what happens here...and with me."

"Sounds like a plan. What are you up to for the rest of the day?"

"Going for a drive. Want to come along?"

I answer in the affirmative. First he wants to drive over the pass for a view down the other side. I suggest finding Barns and getting him to cover the ground in his Huey, but Emerson prefers to drive.

"Who knows how much longer I'll be able too? Hell's bells, I've covered nearly every passable road from Quang Tri to Chu Lai and inland also, at times nearly to the A Shau. Mind you that was a couple of years ago. I'm not looking to get shot.

His old Renault is parked just down the street so after he has a few words with Chi we jump in and leave, heading north. We pass Red Beach which was halfway between Da Nang and Hai Van Pass, and I ask him to pull over for a minute.

"Why here?" he exclaims.

I tell him I'd like to look over the beach towards Da Nang Bay and contemplate for a moment what's happened in this country since the Marines landed on this very spot in March of '65. Emerson immediately begins to get angry.

"You know what the fuck happened. You guys moved in 'en masse' and proceeded to ruin the country, not to mention killing who knows how many people. Probably millions. But I get your drift. Who could have imagined back then, the volume of bombs and the extent of destruction?"

"Not me. I was 'in country' when they landed. Just getting to learn the ropes. I heard the reports on Armed Forces Radio as it happened. Had a little Sony and was sitting on the Continental Shelf looking over the square enjoying a morning beer. It's hotter down there that time of year than it is up this way. At any rate, the radio announcer was likening it to D Day. But later on the Armed Forces TV showed local girls meeting them as they stepped off the landing craft, draping lei's around their necks. Pretty weird, especially thinking that the Marines went from that to Khe Sanh and Con Thien."

After that I'm expecting Emerson to begin again on the treatment of the locals, the destruction of their houses and farms, his same old mantra. But instead he enlightens me.

"I will say that the Marines had the one good option that I know of which was succeeding with the local people. The Combined Action Program."

"I've heard of it but fill me in."

"They'd place a rifle squad and a medic in a village who worked with the local militia that was made up of males too young or two old to be in either army. They'd pick the type of marine that could get along with the locals. You know how many of these American kids were. The 'gook syndrome'. Obviously that type wasn't used. Maybe boys off the farm were most effective. At any rate, they and their militia partners, along with the villagers would eventually establish a good rapport, mostly keeping them on our side without the napalming and the bombing."

Emerson stops for a moment because climbing the pass requires paying attention especially with the traffic coming our way this morning. Much of it is head on and you have to hug a shoulder faster than hell to avoid being creamed.

"That fucker almost got us," said Emerson. "Anyhow because the village was secure from both armies, with a medic living in, things looked good. There were cases of pigs being imported to improve the farm output. Really, just people acting like human beings. You'd be surprised how far that can go."

I begin thinking that these guys were the lucky ones considering that Khe Sanh and Con Thien were the option. We approach the high point of the pass where we'd always stop at the stand for a coke or iced coffee.

"Come on Emerson, let's pull over and walk around. You can climb up above the pill boxes for a good view down the other side if this is as far as we're traveling this morning. I'll get us some drinks."

He starts climbing and I walk over to the stand where I run into Van Ly and Omar slurping over their bowls of morning pho.

"Hey, what's going on with you two…some kind of secret romance?"

"Never happen my captain," says Omar as Van Ly looks at me, without smiling.

"Not a joke Captain Winslow," she interjects. "I have trouble and Omar is helping me."

She begins by saying that they are here expecting to meet with a car full of her relatives from Hue, making it down to Da Nang, figuring that early is better than later if a last minute escape is required. Just to be on the safe side. It turns out that Omar has borrowed an ARVN jeep to make the run up here and they are hoping that whoever shows up will fit in the back. Four or five at most. I tell Van Ly that we can fit at least three in the back of the Renault if they come soon. Emerson has a stop in Tien Phuoc that has to be made before dark, and I hope to go along if nothing else comes up. He makes it back and I relay my Van Ly invitation to him. As usual he's in a rush and in no mood to wait…for anything.

"Ok, I'll hang around for half an hour but that's it. No time. If we miss, I'm sure they can pick up with someone else who's going back to town."

They're lucky. By the time Emerson finishes his iced coffee, an old Citroen pulls in with the back seat full of seven people who are either friends or relatives of Van Ly. Between both vehicles we make them fit and cruise back down through the pass. A quick drop and we're on our way to Tien Phuoc. I'm not sure what the mission is but know that I'll get an earful on the road there.

"So what is it my old friend. What's up?" I know it's something out of the ordinary from the way he's acting.

We're driving along a narrow road that rises to the countryside where some of the best pepper in the world was grown. Tien Phuoc is famous for it.

He smiles, then comes clean.

"She's an old girlfriend. Not so old really but a secret love that had to be severed. I mean, I love Chi and want to marry her. In fact, we are married legally as far as the US is concerned, but not Vietnamese. Visas and tickets come first. You know how that is. No, this girl is Hiep Le and I was so smitten with her that there was no way to recuse myself….if that's the word."

"It isn't." I tell him, "but go on."

"I was up here building a schoolhouse in the countryside two years ago and she was the teacher. You'll understand when you meet her. Just beautiful…inside and out. Plus, a sexual dynamo. Fuck it man, I know that I should be living to a higher standard running the IVS office and all, but I'm weak. I have no excuses. And I felt bad about Chi for the duration of my whole affair with Hiep, which is why I finally broke it off, I couldn't handle the guilt. Not to mention that it wasn't doing anything for Hiep. Where could it go?"

"Then why the hell are we heading up to see her today?"

"Just a quick trip. I need to leave her with some cash. She'll never leave this country no matter who's the boss, and I'd like to think I can do the right thing when push comes to shove."

Well, that makes sense. The countryside up this way is beautiful. Some rolling hills, a very pleasant winding road through them with occasional houses and small hamlets seemingly untouched by US bombing. They've been lucky, or it has been rebuilt. Either way a pleasant country for an afternoon's drive. Plus, I'm always up for meeting another beautiful woman.

"She lives just up the road here, not in the village. An old woman lives with her, but I was never able to identify her as a relative or a servant. It's a small house and love making required a certain discreetness which we quickly mastered. Lucky for us the old woman is deaf or almost deaf."

We drive on a short distance in silence until Emerson pulls off the road in front of a small ordinary country house. An old woman was sitting out front. She recognized Emerson as he opened the car door and ran into the house. As we approached the front porch a young woman stepped out and waved, with a large smile on her face. She is stunning. Emerson remains silent, then steps up on the porch deck and gives her a hug that holds for several moments. When he steps back, he introduces us.

"Glad to meet you Captain Winslow," she tells me with a smile on her face. "I don't see so many American officers these days."

I return her greetings and sit where she beckons me on the porch beside the old woman who has retaken her seat. Emerson accompanies Hiep inside. I attempt conversation with the old one however my interpretation of Vietnamese is not to her liking though she does appear to hear what I'm saying. Perhaps she isn't that deaf. Perhaps my Vietnamese language skills are not of a dialect she is familiar with. Who knows, and what does it matter? We sit enjoying the view of the pepper vines across the road. Some are on frames and others are growing up a tree I'm not familiar with. Presently Hiep and Emerson return to the deck with tea and cookies. We sit awhile longer, chatting politely and finishing the refreshments before taking our leave.

"I'm so sorry we did not have time to know each other better Captain Winslow, but Emerson says he must be back in Da Nang before darkness sets in and I understand that. We wouldn't want him or you to be captured by the dreaded VC, would we." Another beautiful smile as we return to the car for the return trip which proves to be uneventful.

"Why don't you drop me off at the air base" I ask. "I'm hungry and might meet up with Peters or Everest or even Barns at the mess. If you'd like, come with me. No one gives a damn any more."

"Thanks Ed, but Chi will be waiting for me at the office. We have an evening meal together most days and that would be, let's say, more than proper tonight. Thanks for keeping me company."

"Thanks for the ride," I answered, "and thanks for introducing me to Hiep, and filling me in on an 'age-old story'. Catch you later at the Bamboo if you 're interested. I need to check with Van Ly to see that things worked out."

He drops me at the main gate, and I walk to the mess. Luckily there are still enough Americans on this site that they supply the cooks and the food. I'm starving considering we haven't eaten since morning, the day's been such a rush. I meet Major Barns in the chow line which isn't long.

"Where you been Ed? We need to catch up but let's pile on the food first."

Believe it or not, good roast beef with dehydrated potatoes, reconstituted and fried, along with canned string beans are great. Never had a better meal.

"I've had better" says Barns, "but this works and I'm damn grateful… however there are things happening that we need to address ."

I fill him in on our trip to the top of Hai Van Pass earlier in the day which indicated some kind of mass exodus from Hue and points north very soon and he agrees.

"General Luong is very worried. He is in no position to face captivity by forces from the North, knowing his mission is to remain and continue with his command. Reports have funneled back to him of major officers abandoning their troops on the field and fleeing out of the country to Bangkok or Hong Kong. Apparently, that kind of desertion is not yet widespread but indications are that it could be sooner than later. What next?"

"Have you seen Everest, or Peters? They both seem to be on the in when it comes to immediate intelligence."

My immediate thought is about visas for Lien and myself for Australia which I have neglected for the past couple of days.

"I haven't seen either of them" is Barns' reply. "Last chance today would be the Bamboo. How about it? My jeep is outside."

"Let's get going, man".

Barns and I walked in after dark. The Bamboo is crowded with US Military, ex-pats, ARVN, hustlers, girlfriends and short time girls. I'm concerned about the success of Van Ly's day. She and Lien plus the new girl Khanh are behind the bar and very busy. When they catch up, I wave Van Ly over.

"How did it all work out?" I asked. "Did you get them all settled in safely?"

"They are all taken care of. In friends' houses that are safe for now. I worry about other family and friends in Hue. They remember the killings by the NVA after the Tet of '68. Even some that were on their side were killed. Anger at collaborators can be very fierce and unreasonable. They also remember killings by teams of the so called Phoenix Program from your army. Both sides kill us."

I tried to reason that those days were gone, at least on our side. All available intelligence indicates that the move when it comes will be a push towards Saigon to end the war. Retaliation, if any, will occur after the army is victorious.

"Maybe you don't see Captain Ed, but I am very cautious around your friend Lt. Arthur Everest. I know that he was part of the Phoenix killer groups that worked in the Hue vicinity three or four years ago. He scares me for I know what he can… what he did do."

I understand her fears which certainly are legitimate. In wars civilians are fucked. They have to pick a side to survive. They make the best choice they can and if it's the losing side, look out. A really impossible position to be in and I'm trying to make that point with Van Ly.

"What you say is right, but I still very afraid of Lt. Everest. He bad man. He kill Vietnamese people who not be in army. Very bad."

"Listen Van Ly. No need to worry about that any longer. Americans are mostly gone. Lt. Everest does only scouting trips to find out information."

I of course have no idea if that statement is correct. Who the hell knows what he's doing? She begins to get busy along with the others, so I amble to the back deck where Omar is sitting looking out over the water where the fishing boats have lit up the area. I assume he is still mulling over his predicament or rather his family's predicament in Saigon. The half dozen empty beer cans on the table in front of him indicate that he'll be somewhat mellowed out.

"How you be Captain? You make it back Da Nang before me."

I mention the run to Tien Phuoc and he asks if we'd seen any military activity along that route.

"Something is in the wind, and I have to make a decision soon. Do you think your friend Signor at the Consulate can help me get my family out if it comes to that?"

I assure him that things will work out in his favor, not quite knowing if that in fact is correct. Omar knows American's well enough to be skeptical, or in fact to not even be a believer. Then without any fanfare he leaves to spend the night with his girlfriend, and I can't blame him, for I hoped to do the same.

Barns steps out informing me that one of the flyboys inside from the AFVN had been flying north of Quang Tri in an A-37 and spotted tanks on Route 1. They were Russian T-34s.

"According to Peters that area has been contested for the last couple of years so perhaps that's not an immediate worry," I mention.

"Maybe, but I wouldn't bet my life on it. We've gotta get our shit together and fast."

I revert back to thinking I also have to do just that, and my first move should be to get back to Saigon pronto with passports to pick up those Australian visas from Sandy.

Just then Banks, the door gunner and mechanic who has half recovered from his wounds, runs back towards us to relay a message to his aircraft commander.

"You won't believe it Major but they're both down."

"Who are you talking about Banks? Who's down?"

"Lt. Everest and Capt. Peters. They were both scouting out towards the A Shau with an ARVN company in a Huey and it went down. The Captain Peters radioed in after a crash landing saying that he was just banged up but Everest might be more serious. He was just coming around. Two of the ARVN soldiers were killed. Ditto copilot and one gunner."

"What's the plan," exclaims Barns, "or is there one?"

"General Luong says it's too risky to send out a bird tonight. It's pitch dark and ground fire is unknown. Peters thought they'd be ok till morning. Then they hope it's us that can go in for an extraction."

This takes the edge off the evening. It finishes the evening. They both leave soon after. I told them I'd be there early too and join the crew on the flight in. Of course, we didn't know what the morning would hold or what orders might come down by then. I leave soon after with Lien and I explain the situation and tell her I'll be leaving to join up early in the morning.

"I wish you stay with me my Ed. Maybe you die." She is worried and has reason to.

We are airborne at the crack of dawn, heading for the area last reported to be the location of the downed Huey. It's an uncertain fix though Barns s accustomed to that type of situation. He's been at it for years. One other ARVN trooper is with me in the rear. Reports do not indicate how many will be returning...alive or bagged. I'm nervous. Lien is right. We're too close to the end.

The signal from Peters' radio is weak so it's difficult for Barns to site the downed chopper. In the end he requests they pop smoke, thinking that he'll drop in one way or the other, hot with his gunners on the lookout. I'm sitting on the floor with my feet on the skids scanning the right of the machine and spot it first. After signaling Barns I climb back inside and strapped myself in on a seat. He's able to bring the Huey in quite close to the downed machine. There's no fire from the ground thus far. The Viet soldier jumps out with me, and we run towards Peterson who is on his feet helping Everest. The two pilots are injured but ambulatory. The gunner and one soldier had been crushed when the bird rolled up on its side after skidding in. They're both goners. Eventually living, wounded and dead are on board but as we're lifting off AK fire erupted from an area behind the downed aircraft The gunners are able to suppress fire until we have gained enough altitude to be safe.

Everest has a mean gash on his head and apparently was dazed or unconscious most of the night however he is coming around. Looked like he'll be ok in a couple of days. What could have been a disaster has proven to be a rather uneventful operation. After landing and getting the wounded to an aid station, I ask Peters what they had been up to when the chopper went down.

"Well, Everest has two ARVN Airborne Rangers on his team, and they were suspicious of a certain area, so he thought since a chopper was available, we'd check it out. We found nothing, but they obviously found us. You know the rest."

"Let's play it safe man, and we might be lucky enough to make it back for a sail with you around Cape Cod."

Peters smiles, then leaves for the aid station to check on Everest. I make a quick trip back to Lien's and my pad to pick up passports and catch the mid-day Air America Volpar to Saigon.

CHAPTER 22:

SAIGON... AGAIN

A JEEP DROPS ME OFF AT THE CORNER OF LE LOI AND TU Do at the door of Girval Cafe. Street urchins and beggars converge for the kill, but I brush them aside and enter. The place is half full of Vietnamese politicians from the Assembly which is based in the old Opera House across the square, the seat of power. Girval is rumored to be the location where most of the conspiracies that had felled various governments over the years of the Republic of Vietnam's existence.

After ordering a cold 33 I grab a seat by the window overlooking Tu Do across from the Continental Hotel. The hotel's open terrace is nearly full. Correspondents, TV people, French planters and businessmen, beautiful women in company or waiting for their assignation are all in place. Business as usual on a hot Saigon afternoon. I look up as Sandy walks in, comes over and joins me as if we had a scheduled meeting.

"Saw you walk in from the Shelf and figured you might be looking for me. Just out having an afternoon drink with a new girl. Quite fancy she is."

"Aren't they all," I reply.

"Most of 'em mate, you've got that right. I assume you're here for those visas. I've got it set up, and if you've your passports with you it will be a done deal in less than an hour."

I hand them over and we agree to meet up at the Kangaroo in an hour. My intention is to walk around the square, stop in at the bar and wait there in good company. He leaves and I begin the walk I've made a hundred times, heading towards the river on Tu Do St. Past the opera house and the Caravelle Hotel. I'd recently learned it had been named after the Caravelle jet transport that Air France had placed in service in 1959 when the hotel first opened. Air France had been an investor in the project and its offices remain on the ground floor that corners on Tu Do.

For me, the routine walk towards the river is an escape from my present world in Da Nang. I'd walked it so many times during my tours in the mid-sixties that it feels more familiar than my back yard in the States. I'd run into all kinds of people. US military, ARVN, embassy types, grifters, journalists, whores and shoeshine boys. As well as contractors, pimps. perverts and criminals. All of them pursuing their own hustle.

"You want young girl?" one of the shoeshine boys asks me. He must figure my shoes don't need a shine, or I'm not the type who has time for that kind of wasted effort.

"Never happen" I tell him. "Go home to your mother."

"Number ten fuck you GI," is his reply.

I sigh and walk on, after waving him off.

I continue past Sean Flynn's old hangout which he or one of his cohorts had named Frankie's Place. Then numerous shops, bars and hotels till reaching the river where the still quite grand Majestic Hotel sits on the corner. The identical place where Graham Greene's character Fowler, watched fighter planes being unloaded from an American aircraft carrier in the early Fifties, back when this failing war was in its infancy and when this street was the Rue Catinat in the days of French Colonialism. My mind is turning to Lien, and what tomorrow might bring.

"Good to see you Captain Ed. What would you like to drink?" It's Tot at the Kangaroo, where I've made it to on the return walk up Nguyen Hue St.

"Good to be here again Tot. A 33 would be fine. I'm waiting for Sandy who should be here soon."

Khanh comes over and sits down on the stool beside me. I order her a Saigon Tea and she fills me in on her plan of also moving to Australia with a recent boyfriend who has fallen in love with her.

"That sounds like a great idea, but isn't this quite sudden?"

"It be very sudden and just in time, don't you think."

I smile at that and admit that it's happening just in time.

"Lucky girl Khanh. Maybe we fly out together with my Lien if Sandy has our passports."

Just then he walks in, and overhearing says, "it's a done deal mate. All stamped, signed and sealed. Catch a plane out of here and you both should be home free."

"Thank you, Sandy, a thousand times over. I'll never be able to repay you."

"A cold beer will do and something else. Word had just come in at the embassy that NVA troops were reported heading from the highlands towards Chu Lai and furthermore, tanks were reported crossing the DMZ. Don't hang around here too long Captain."

I indicate that my flight up north is arranged as long as I make it to the Air America hangar at Tan Son Nhut in time.

However, I'm good for another beer with you. Who knows, might be our last."

"Maybe so, but before you leave listen to this."

I order another round and he begins.

"This morning I accompanied our Ambassador, Geoffrey Price to your embassy so that he could have a talk with your man Graham Martin. We were waiting in the anteroom outside of his office when Price was called into another office for something or other. I remained where I was and was having a conversation with the Marine security guard when who walked in but Ed Daly, the owner of World Airways. You know about him?"

"I know who he is and that he is a hard drinking, tough Irish bastard. Is that what you mean?"

"Well, it seems that Daly has a contract with the federal government to fly refugees from Da Nang to Saigon and apparently Martin has put a stop to these flights. Daly doesn't like it. The Marine stops him from entering the office. Daly has a gun in a shoulder holster and tries to barge in. The Marine stops him and says, "keep it up Daly and I'll blow your fucking head off." That doesn't deter Daly. He tells the guard that he has a contract to fulfill and is going to live up to it. Tells him that he is going to fly to Da Nang one way of the other and 'fuck all you guys.' Then he barges right into Martin's office with the Marine following. I stand up and watch through the doorway, then see Martin look up from whatever he's doing. I'll recount things the best that I can."

It's approaching the hour that I should head for the airport but I in no way wanted to miss the rest of Sandy's story.

"Daly, give your gun to the guard and perhaps I'll talk to you, if I must. I'm sure you're aware that I could have you locked up for this kind of behavior."

Daly says, "I'm aware of that sir," and hands his pistol to the marine. Then he says, "and you can turn off the god damn tapes too."

Martin says, "they're off Daly and what is it that prompts this uncalled for rude behavior?"

"I've been told that no more clearances will be given to World Airways flights to Da Nang with no explanation. Not that I would accept one. I've a legal written contract authorizing these flights that you're damn sure aware of. Why the bullshit? People could be dying."

"Let me try and explain a few things to you Daly. First of all, I run things in this country regarding anything USA. I've determined, actually we've determined, Polger from the CIA is with me on this, that more flights might be dangerous to your planes and pilots and anyone on board. There's a secondary motive. This kind of thing could very likely encourage a panic among the people up there and we don't want that happening."

"If they panic it will be because they know they should. It won't be up to any American. I'm afraid that will be a Vietnamese issue," was Daly's reply."

"Listen Daly, stay on the ramp and all will be ok. If things change, you'll be informed. If you do leave, they might shoot you down and I would be in complete agreement."

"All I can say Ambassador is that there won't be that many more days that we have this option. Give it some thought. I'll sit tight for a day or two. Then I might have to reassess."

That was the end of Sandy's story, and it possibly could affect me. Who knew how many options would be there when it came down to the wire?

I express my goodbyes to Sandy, Tot and Khanh, wishing them all the best. Who knew how it was all going to go down in Saigon, or when? Perhaps I'd never see any of them again.

Luckily the ride to the airport is unobstructed and uneventful and the plane's just loading. By this time, I was friends with the pilot Lee Mullins, who'd been with Air America since Laos, ten years ago. He waved me on board from the cockpit, and we're off.

One more time, I'm back in the Bamboo by ten o'clock for my favorite late-night drink. Van Ly begins pouring my Courvoisier as she sees me walk through the door. I smile greetings. The bar was unusually crowded. I ask Van Ly what's going on and where might Lien be.

"Lien will be here soon. She was helping one of my relatives with a problem. The bar is full because nobody knows."

I ask her just what that means, 'nobody knows'. What is it that nobody knows?

"Tanks are passing through Quang Tri. NVA tanks. This time it be forever. They will not return to the North. I know because another cousin came here today who was in touch with his uncle who is with the Liberation Front, and he knows. They have had the final order to make the push South. Nobody knows what will happen, or when."

I tell her that I'd heard something like that from Sandy in Saigon. They'd met a few months earlier when he'd been in Da Nang for some business with Wales Signor in the Consulate. At any rate the stories seemed to mesh, as little as I had at the moment. After looking around I can see that they are all here, even General Luong, who I am sure has never been in this building. It's beneath a General of the armed forces of the Republic of Vietnam. Barns comes towards me at the bar, and I can see Peterson and Everest talking over at a corner table. Omar and Banks are playing pool. The thing is, we've all been tossing what appears to be impending doom, around for the last month and haven't made a plan. To my knowledge General Luong doesn't have a plan. So we'll see…and Barns is first.

"I see you made it back," Barns says. "Success? You have the visas?"

"I sure as hell do. Old Sandy came through with flying colors. Lien and I are good to go whenever. All we need are tickets and who knows about that. Still down the road a ways."

"Maybe not that far. I'm sure you've heard the latest."

"Maybe. I've heard Sandy's info from the Aussi embassy, as well as Van Ly. That's it but I can surmise. We all know the territory."

"I'll tell you something Ed. Let this thing drag on awhile. Last night I curled up with Khanh. Man, I couldn't believe it. It'd been a while for me, but we went it for most of the night regardless. I think maybe I love her… GI."

He smiles at me, sheepishly, for he did not normally use that type of language. I mean after all, we are officers.

"She is one wild fuck, I'll tell you that. I'd really like to stick around here a while longer. Hell, I've been here for years. I'm owed a couple of months of sexual bliss, and why the hell not?"

"That my friend will not be up to you. Have you picked up anything from Peterson or Everest? They always think they are in the know earlier than anyone else. But I'll tell you something. Having had long experience with the girls from Tam Hiep I'd guess that Van Ly might be a more accurate source."

He nodded and said we'd need to have a talk with our fellow officers before last call, which looked to be some hours away. The fact that the four of us ended up here is quite an anomaly for there are supposed to be no Americans still fighting in Viet Nam. We of course are under the radar. We are from different commands and possess some cover from the US Embassy in Saigon through the consulate here. Wales Signor is legitimate. We are not. But if you look through the history of this war, you'll find it crowded with our type of character. Shady, possibly illegal, but plugging away with the program. And who cares at this point, for the program has failed.

I see Art Everest wave Barns over to join him and Peterson, so I tag along. Barns begins.

"So, what is it? The end near. I've heard tanks are heading south between Quang Tri and the DMZ."

"So they say," reveals Len Peterson, "however we expect to hold them off at the pass." Then he laughs like hell. "I'm kidding of course. That won't happen unless the 1st Cav. shows up...on horseback."

"Quit dreaming," says Barns, stifling a laugh, "no one's going to show up, including the great South Vietnamese army. Let's face it, they're burned out, we're burned out. The whole fucking country is burned out, and I'd bet the North is too. Let's call a truce and settle things over a good bottle of bourbon." He turned and ordered another round from Van Ly.

"I love bourbon," said Everest, "but not diluted with that filthy coke which is a drink for heathens. For me it's Turkey on ice. I prefer crushed ice which enhances the taste."

He calls to Van Ly to change his drink. She brings over three 'whiskey cokes' telling the 'great Seal' she'll be back with his.

"I have Wild Turkey under bar. Be back in a minuet….with crushed ice. Big tip for me." She smiles, walking away knowing Lt. Everest will do just that. He's after her ass too and she knows it, and she also knows that he's barking up the wrong tree. Her ass will remain a mystery.

The Turkey shows up and the boys are drinking up. Three captains and a major, all about the same age but outranked by Maj. Barns. He had easily made that rank being a pilot with four tours. No one is sure how many Everest has due to a certain secrecy among Navy Seal Teams. Of course, nothing like that mattered anymore, especially among these four American officers.

"Listen," Barns articulates, "why are we talking like this? When it happens, it happens. We know we're going to make it to Saigon so let it go. What we should do is see where General Luong stands."

"Do you mean 'when is he going to jump ship'," interjects Peters. "Reports are that that's what happened in the Central Highlands. The near riot on the choked highway between Pleiku and Qui Nhon happened because the officers in charge of the ARVN disappeared. They flew out to Saigon hoping to catch a plane out of the country early. Meaning before Saigon falls. That's where their heads are according to my source."

"Let's ask the general directly. I know him to be an honorable man and can't believe he'd 'jump ship' with the rest of them."

Capt. Peters leaves to talk with General Luong. Soon they both return to the table.

The Americans all stand up as the general approached them. He smiles, nod towards is. then takes a seat.

"Could you ask the girl to bring me a glass of vodka please," he says to no one in particular. Pleasantries are made while we wait for Van Ly to return with his drink. She's prompt and he begins talking before any of the American officers can ask questions.

"General Truong is in Saigon having a conference with President Thieu who wants to abandon the northern provinces and pull the troops down to defend Saigon. He and I think this is a crazy move and hope to persuade the President otherwise."

"General, how can the president of this country be thinking along those lines?" asks Everest who is the kind of guy who would never give up. It could be said that he is a very principled Navy Seal.

Actually, we are all astonished to know that it has come this far, even considering that that's all we've been talking about all evening.

"I think we all know that we will not prevail. I have felt that ever since the Americans essentially 'left us to the lions' in '73. It was not just that we needed their support, militarily and otherwise. We needed them to make us a functioning country. We were never able to develop the feeling that we Vietnamese in the South, could be our own country, the country of the Republic of Vietnam, without the American presence, and of course American money. In the end we, all of us are Vietnamese; North, Central and South. What can I say? When I was young, I favored the Viet Minh who were fighting the French. I worked with the French, but I was not of them. I was with the other side, and I believe most of us that were not making a living or finding a source of power with the European country had similar feelings."

I could see where he was coming from. When you look back a few years, the DMZ was just a dividing line for two years so people could return to their residence of preference or relocate according to their wishes. Then there would be an election for the presidency. Foreseeing the results, the Americans decided to form the Republic of Vietnam south of that line of demarcation and go with it. Build a country of the half with whoever lived there. I think the basic problem was that a good portion of the people who lived there thought of Vietnam as a whole and this concept was always foreign to them. It never developed the heart and soul and the cohesiveness that makes a country a country. It's my observation, not to say everyone feels this way, but after my years here, I sense something along these lines.

Van Ly is delivering another round of drinks ordered by someone or she just figured she'd get with it.

"Thank you my beautiful one," says Everest. She nods with a half-smile and returns to her bar.

"General," asks Everest, "do you actually believe that that is going to be the result? The whole of I Corps will be abandoned to the North. Da Nang is the biggest military installation in the country. There is the main Da Nang Air Base, the one at Marble Mountain, and four port facilities and storage facilities for tens of thousands of supplies, fuel and ammunition. How can it be abandoned? What about the tanks, aircraft, ships, field guns and whatever? The North will be supplied for years."

"I'm thinking that General Truong will reorganize and redeploy the troops in I Corps to a better defensive position, in part because it might stall off the North and it might convince Thieu to at least postpone the abandon-ment of this whole sector."

I ask the general what his personal position is, and he is quite straightforward

"As you have probably heard, some of my contemporaries have aban-doned their command in the field and fled the country. I will keep my com-mand here until I am ordered elsewhere. If in the end I am in Saigon and it's hopeless, I will try to leave with my family since I have no idea how ex officers in the ARVN will be treated by the winners, but I will expect the worst. So, I don't really have a choice. I must take care of my family first."

After hearing that I let him know that I'd do the same and expect to, though it is just Lien and myself. General Luong excuses himself, leaving for the base. The rest of us sit there in silence lost in thought.

CHAPTER 23:

NVA CAMP...
A SHAU

CAPTAIN BAO HAS RETURNED TO CAMP AFTER A MAJOR briefing with the top brass of the NVA. He is bringing Sgt. Chanh up to date on what is expected to be the course of action in the next few days.

"This operation may begin earlier than expected if the ARVN defenses fall apart as some of the main top officers of our army suspect. We will see but I think it might go that way because of intelligence from the local force regiments. Most of those fighters have friends and relatives among the local populations. Reports indicate more war weariness among that population, than we are experiencing among our troops." He hesitated for a moment with a sly smile finishing with "hopefully more war weariness than you and I are experiencing."

Chanh assured him that he would last until the end and is sure that Capt. Bao will too.

"Most of my troops are green, like Privates Cuong and Huu Considering that we have not fought the kind of battle against the puppet troops where casualties were immense, they don't have a feeling for what a nasty, dirty experience war can be. Private Huu is anxious to be among the victors when we march into Saigon. He's set to go, as are most of my young troops. It's just the old boys like us who are skeptical. We know how easy it is to die. Anytime, from anything. I'd like to make it back home for a normal life so am going to be careful, but will do my duty, however difficult it may be."

Capt. Bao explained that this unit could be sent in early to cut Highway 1 at Hai Van Pass so that ARVN units from Hue would not be able reach Da Nang for reinforcements and resupply. Units were being sent to encircle and eventually capture Phu Bai Airport also which would prevent any reinforcements or resupply by air. Then there was also the possibility that they'd be sent south to Tien Phuoc to knock out the ARVN Battalion stationed there so that that Route 1 could be cut between Da Nang and Chu Lai. He wasn't sure what he'd prefer for his men.

"I'd like to take on Tien Phuoc," said Sgt. Chanh. "It's a longer march but you know the terrain necessary to cross to reach the top of Hai Van Pass. Very difficult and my green troops would be slow to acclimate. Then again, it's twice as far. We might have trucks to carry us halfway to the pass. That road is still passible, if just barely."

"Why worry sergeant, when we can let the big shots do that. We will follow the order when it comes down without complaint as we are wont to do. It's gotten us this far. Can you fucking believe it's been ten years? A miracle we're still alive."

It was nearing chow time, so Chanh went back to his platoon's bunker to eat with the men. He always enjoyed his conversations with Huu and Cuong, though Huu was the more talkative. The food had been improving for some reason. Must be the cooks for the substance hadn't changed. Rice, nuoc mam, scavenged vegetables, noodles, and on occasion canned meat from Russia or China. Good fare for an army that had scraped by on next to nothing for years.

"Good food," said Huu, "almost as good as my mother back in the village."

"You're full of shit," Cuong came back with, "my mother can cook a thousand times better than these army guys."

Chanh was ignoring them. He was dreaming how an evening meal with Hoa back in Thai Nguyen would be about now. Then the clerk from the company headquarters came by with word for Chanh to stop in to see Capt. Bao immediately. He dropped from his dream to reality and walked back to see the captain.

"Another messenger has come in," said Capt. Bao, " with word that Gen. Dung has taken over the military leadership from the great Giap and there is a report that Le Duc Tho himself is down in Loc Ninh at COMITON headquarters. Apparently, he rode in on a motor bike by himself. This must be it, the beginning of the end."

The two men entered a discussion on what might be coming next, going over their previous conversation. Then another messenger rode in. He handed off his packet to Chanh, and Capt. Bao asked him to open and read it out loud. Chanh is wide eyed and says,

"You won't believe this captain. Hue has fallen without a fight. The puppet troops have all fled in a panic. Their leaders have disappeared and there is a mass exodus toward Da Nang."

"This is hard to believe sergeant. When you think how hard they fought for that city during the Tet of '68 and again during the Spring Offensive of 1972, why would they abandon it so easily?"

"Well, as we heard earlier, it appears that their leaders did leave their troops on the field. Apparently, the whole thing just fell apart. And supposedly Thieu has ordered the central highlands evacuated. Looks good for us, Captain Bao."

Captain Bao issued orders for the men to prepare for departure at a moment's notice. He had nothing specific in the way of orders but expected them by morning. Chanh went back to his station to prep his men.

"Private Huu, where is Cuong? I haven't seen him all day. For over a day actually."

Huu was hesitant but not for long. His sergeant wouldn't accept that. "Cong has a girlfriend and left to see her last night and so far, hasn't returned. I'm sure he will be in soon."

"How the hell did he find a girlfriend out here" asked Sergeant Chanh. "There aren't any."

"If you look, you can find, " said Huu, "and Private Huu looked. You know we sometimes buy food from the local Katu people. Half of them are girls, so that be your answer."

"No insubordination from you private," was Chanh's response. "He'd better show his ass up here soon or I'll have it."

He impressed on the men that this was serious, that tomorrow would be the beginning of the greatest happening of their life. And possibly the most dangerous. Some of us won't be returning home. So pack up, prepare for departure and get a good night's sleep.

There is mass panic on the outskirts of Hue. It isn't just the civilians who fear the unexpected. There is an unruly crowd of ARVN soldiers whose units have fallen into disarray and who obviously hope to escape south. Many of these soldiers' families have accompanied them north as is customary in this army and they too are fleeing with them…where to, they have no idea.

This mass of humanity is pouring south toward Da Nang. Vehicles of every description fill the highway: black Citroens from the '40s, civilian buses, cars, trucks. US army jeeps, APCs, cyclos, ox carts. Anything on wheels, all loaded to overflowing.

The refugees are packing their worldly goods. Suitcases, TVs, cooking pots, furniture, baskets of fruit.

The majority are ARVN soldiers and their families. Some have stripped their uniforms of insignia, some their uniforms altogether, but not their arms. It's an out-of-control mob.

North at the DMZ, regulars of the invading army of North Viet Nam are pouring into the land of their southern brothers.

Columns of soldiers, Russian tanks and APCs. Chinese duce & a halfs loaded with troops.

It is a convoy that faces no opposition, needs no guards, and is viewed only by the few farmers that have stuck with their land. Opposition forces seem to have vanished. The coast is clear.

Chanh and his soldiers are breaking camp at the old A Shau US Special Forces site near the southern end of the valley where they have lived for months. Orders have been received for them to begin marching on the road that leads to Da Nang where they will help to secure the air base that is occupied by the air force of the Republic of Viet Nam and other various ARVN units along with a small contingent of US advisors and contractors.

Sgt. Chanh has completed a conference with Captain Bao and is prepping his troops for the march.

"You men will be marching for a number of kilometers. We expect truck transport for part of the trip but that will depend on how smoothly this operation moves forward. We will not be alone on this march. Other units will be using the same route in areas as well as support and supply vehicles. We will see."

"Sgt. Chanh" said Huu. "What do you expect along the way? What will happen when we arrive at the Da Nang air base?"

"Perhaps we fight, perhaps we have an easy time with no opposition, perhaps we die. Who can say? We will stay organized as you have all been taught and as we have been for the time I have been your sergeant. We will have a successful war."

CHAPTER 24:

THE BAMBOO,

DA NANG

THERE IS A CONSTANT BUZZ THROUGHOUT THE CROWDED
bar, and the whiskey is flowing. I'm talking with Omar who is still worried
about his wife and kids in Saigon.

"Don't worry Omar, we'll save you," I tell him.

"I know you can say," he replies, "but maybe you cannot do."

"You may be right on that Omar however Wales Signor from the consulate will be here later on and I will make certain that he arranges transport
for you in time to escape a total collapse if indeed it appears that that is going
to happen."

Once again I'm hoping I am right. We...the US owes Omar. He's been
a faithful interpreter for our units till they all left and is still filling the same
slot now with the ARVN. And he's a good friend.

Van Ly returns with another round and asks to talk with me alone, so
I move to the end of the bar. Omar rejoins the pool table crew.

"It's beginning to look like the end will happen, and that it is near," Captain Ed. "Be sure that plans for Lien and yourself are fixed and solid. I have heard from the top that plans are in effect to take the whole country. It was unexpected, even for them. They had no idea that the substance of the South was so weak. The rush is on."

"What about Emerson Fitz, Van Ly. He tells me he is staying till the end but must get Chi out soon. Have you seen her…or him?"

"I don't know" she answered. "But here he is now, You ask him. I'll will bring you another drink. It be Wild Turkey for you, and a 33 for him."

Before I could thank her Emerson grabs the stool beside me. He looks flushed which is unusual for him for he's seen everything this country can deliver….almost.

"I was able to see Chi off to Saigon today. Just barely. All aircraft leaving were full. Unlike yourself, special favors are difficult for me to acquire. Half of these ARVN think IVS is a communist outfit…just like a number of your compadres. Fucking idiots. Whatever we are, at least we help the people. We don't shoot them."

"So, what happened. Who'd she fly out on?"

"Your buddy Lee Mullins from Air America. We were at the airport utterly defeated and I saw him walking out to the Beech Volpar. Ran over and asked, and he said have her jump in. Said he always had room for a pretty girl. So I'm hoping she's in Saigon right now. She said she'd call me in the morning. Like I told you, I'm not leaving till they throw me out."

"Good for her and I hope you're making the right choice for yourself. These guys coming in will be tough bastards, you can be sure of that."

"You're right Ed and I agree with you, but think about it. How many of us from the outside will stay till the end? Not many I assure you. Maybe a few journalists. But I will."

"I think you're crazy, but fuck it man, go for it. In a way I'd like to do the same, but Lien and I have to leave for a life away from war, the ultimate evil. She deserves a peaceful life."

Emerson decides to return to his office just in case Chi calls tonight. He tosses down his beer and bids good night to Van Ly and me. I'm still hoping that Lien will show up. She's been busy helping people that had left Hue when it was still possible, so I hadn't seen that much of her the last couple of days.

I can see Everest and Peters talking at a corner table and walk over to join them just as Barns walks in so we both pull up a chair. They're working on a half-gallon of PX Early Times bourbon. This is sure to be a long night.

"Who at this table knows more about what's going on than I do, is what I'd like to know," exclaims Barns. "I know you don't Ed but with the spook and the assassin here someone must."

I'm not sure that Peters or Everest appreciates the titles, however they both know which fits whom.

"Haven't cut a throat since last week," interjects Everest. "Some of these ARVN Seal substitutes are better at that than I am. The thing is we don't acquire a great deal of information after that procedure. You'd better ask Len here."

"I don't mean to spy into your business Arthur," puts in Barns, "but why are you cutting throats this late in the game? Who the hell cares who runs the government at this point?"

"You'd be surprised how the military mind functions, Barns. You just fly with it. We have to keep things even, and sometimes that's how we do it."

"What about the info," I ask. "Is it all falling in finally, and if so, how fast."

"I do know one thing," Barns discloses. "The airfield at Phu Bai has been surrounded and captured. I made a quick run up there with a courier and just made it out before they charged through the gates. I don't know about the whole theatre, but from what I've seen and heard no one is putting up much of a fight. There were marines and infantry on that field along with a number of tanks. I radioed back after landing here and was told hardly a shot was fired. Weird."

"The thing is," Len Peters says, "they aren't going to fight. They can see the handwriting on the wall, and it says 'we've lost' so no need being tough and getting shot. There's another issue also. What about after? The ARVN military along with the civilians must manage life with the victors so they play ball. And let's face it. They're brothers. What the fuck are we but interlopers who pushed our shit on them and left when the going got tough. Not that we ever had much of a chance."

Peters pours another round of Early Times which we sip in silence for a few moments of contemplation.

Then he continues with the latest intelligence from above the pass… and south of Da Nang.

"They've cut the roads. We've deciphered from intercepted communication that they've captured over 50,000 ARVN soldiers and well over a hundred tanks and other types of armored vehicles. How's that sound?"

I reply that losses of that magnitude are unbelievable and if true, signify the end for Da Nang. The country will not be far behind.

"And don't forget, the road from Chu Lai to the highlands has also been severed which negates the overland route south. Route 1 in that direction has been closed for at least two days. The only way out of here is by air…or start swimming."

I look up and see that Lien is behind the bar with Van Ly, so excuse myself and make my way through the crowd to see her. Even the mood, from listening in to varied conversations indicates doom. I have to organize my plan for escape with Lien, and soon.

On reaching the bar she exclaims, "I was so worried you'd not be here my Captain. What will we do? Van Ly thinks nothing is fixed."

I hesitate to tell her that Van Ly is correct, but for the moment don't. "I will go to the airport in the morning to make the arrangements. Another question is are you ready to leave. It will be for a long time, possibly forever. You must face that my dear. I know it is hard, but you must come with me to Australia."

"I know in my head that is so, but my heart does not follow so quickly. But do not worry."

Both girls are busy tending to the crowd. My intention is to return to the table with the 'Captains' to resume out conversation but then Wales walks in. He takes the stool next to me and orders a strong vodka tonic.

"I've heard rumors from Saigon that Ambassador Martin and Ed Daly from World Airways nearly got into a fist fight right in the Embassy", said Wales "and am waiting for an update."

"Don't waste your time," I reply, "Sandy gave me the story firsthand. He was just outside the door. It seems Martin was telling Daly that his flights up here were to end. Too dangerous. Actually, Martin was afraid of something going wrong and it would reflect badly on him. Daly blew up. Said he had a contract from the feds and was going to uphold it, no matter Martins opinion."

"Really, are you sure of this? We need him here with his planes. There're a lot of people, military and civilian who need to head south…soon."

"Of course, I'm sure. Sandy was there along with an official from the Australian Embassy. This was a day or so ago. I can't remember now but he hasn't shown up, has he?"

"Fuck no, and like I said we need him."

"You need him…I need him. Lien has to leave for Saigon before all the flights end."

CHAPTER 25:

WORLD AIRWAYS,

DA NANG

I SHOW UP AT THE AIRPORT EARLY ENOUGH TO GRAB EGGS
and coffee at the mess hall with Omar. He has taken it upon himself to find
a return ticket to Saigon.

"Maybe you can do Captain Ed, but I try too. That way maybe one of
us will succeed. I fear for my family."

I tell him I certainly understand and suggest he stick with me. After
all, our missions are identical. Following breakfast, we walk over to the
Air America terminal where Lee Mullins is standing by his over worked
Beechcraft. He's waiting for the CIA bigshots who work out of the Da Nang
consulate that are hightailing it to Saigon. No extra room unfortunately.

"I'd try and pack one more in" said Mullins, "but it's not possible with
the crew I'm carrying this trip. They run everything. Too bad for your friend,
Winslow. Try World when it lands."

I tell Mullins that's why we're here. In short order his passengers show
up and board his plane. He cranks up the machine and makes an immediate

departure on runway 17. Omar and I begin scanning the skies for the World Airways flight.

"I see Captain, coming in from the sea…from the East"

I scan in that direction and finally think I see it coming into view. It looks to be a 727. In short order it circles the field, enters a long approach heading south, then lands on runway 17 which the CIA aircraft had just departed on.

As the World 727 taxis toward the ramp, I detect movement from the Quonset Hut hangars and Revetments that protect the fighter aircraft that line the eastern edge of the large concrete apron.

Hordes of people appear, eventually looking to be in the many hundreds. Then unbelievably come the vehicles. Jeeps, trucks, even a couple of APCs loaded with military and civilian alike, and children. What could they all be thinking?

"They be crazy," said Omar. "What can we do?"

"The first thing Omar, that we will do is sit tight for a minute and think."

I could not have imagined this scenario. Eventually it becomes clear that the majority of this mob, which it now certainly is are ARVN infantry and marines, seemingly desperate to escape any contact with the invading army from the North. What the response will be from that invading army is unknown. Certainly, at this time these forces are in no way prepared to engage those forces in any kind of military action. They are abandoning their posts. Deserting plain and simple.

The 727 has not yet stopped. It taxis slowly past the revetments where AFVN F-5s are tied down. I notice Barnes' Huey parked between two of them, still in one piece. One never knows.

This isn't the first flight by World to Da Nang. They've been flying back and forth to Saigon or Cam Ranh Bay for some days previously according to Wales Signor. The word from the Embassy in Saigon is that the remaining flights will be for women and children only. Apparently, Daly had been assured that the ARVN infantry and marines in this sector would be staying to hold off the NVA and would be fighting to the last man. There had been a lapse of a day which was more than likely caused by the incident relayed to me by Sandy. But here they are with a 727 and it looks as if it's in for some trouble. There's a large number of South Vietnamese troops among the crowd who are not hanging around to confront the NVA. They look to be all about saving their own asses and to hell with everyone else. Including the women and kids.

Omar and I trot out on the ramp towards the aircraft which has slowed to a crawl. I notice that what appears to be mortars are exploding on the far side of the field, thinking that the NVA must be approaching the boundary of the airfield. Time to drag ass.

"You be careful my captain" yells Omar over the din. "These people will trample you, or maybe even shoot you. Keep your pistol handy."

At that moment an ARVN Marine crashes against my side, knocking me to my knees. I'm barely able to struggle to my feet and maintain balance while yelling at him in Vietnamese. He screams back and points his M-16 at my face. I stop and duck until he passes us by.

"Omar yells, "next time they do, you shoot them." If I have to I think to myself.

As the aircraft nearly comes to a stop, two men climb down the rear ramp and enter the crowd. One has a camera. They're pushed aside from the plane. We try to get close enough to the ramp to speak with the man who is helping people struggle aboard while in some cases bashing them with his pistol to fight them off. These are military personnel, not the intended passengers.

A woman carrying a child reaches the first step of the ramp. An ARVN marine pulls her off, slamming her to the pavement. He stands on her head as he climbs aboard himself. As he reaches the top, he's clubbed on the head with a pistol by the man assisting the loading.

These men are all well-armed… angry and panicked. A grenade goes off under one wing. A number of soldiers nearing and climbing up the ramp, look to be members of the Black Panthers, the meanest unit of the 1st ARVN Division.

Omar yells at me again to be careful. He knows these people and that they are dangerous…to everyone. The fucking mob is winning. A man and woman with three kids reach frantically towards the ramp ahead of an ARVN who has a pistol in his hand. He shoots the man, the wife, and then the kids who are immediately trampled by the following mob. The ARVN makes it on the plane.

Omar, who is right beside me screams, "Shoot that bastard. Kill him."

It's too late for that since the soldier has disappeared into the belly of the aircraft. I can see that the wheel wells as well as the baggage compartment are also packed. People are still trying to climb onto the ramp and are attempting to board…all shouting and pushing…soldiers as well as civilians. Others are climbing up on top of the wings and they're falling off. Other military types are firing into the air, over the aircraft attempting to frighten others. Confused and defeated women and children are lying on the ground, sobbing or unconscious. Others from that crowd are trying to lie in front of the wheels. Complete madness.

I look around for Omar who I have lost, then catch sight of him reaching for the ramp. Somehow, he has made it through the crowd. The plane is picking up speed, but he still holds on and is the last one aboard as the World 727 pulls away from the crowd. The mob running after the moving aircraft begins firing at it. A number of grenades are thrown at the aircraft, with one exploding beneath the wing. There is no way the plane can make it to the runway. It appears to be speeding up to attempt a takeoff from the taxiway. I can see the man who had been controlling the ramp from inside, pulling Omar forward, disappearing inside the aircraft. I hope for the best.

The 727 is picking up speed. The left wing tip hits two or three sheds that line the taxiway. The sheds collapse but the plane keeps moving forward, picking up speed. It's nearing the end of the taxiway without initiating a climb. I hold my breath as it slowly rises, barely clearing the airfield fence, but gaining altitude. Moments later it's over the waters of the South China Sea in a steady, shallow climb enroute to Saigon.

I look around at the discouraged mob and the bodies that are left lying on the concrete. People are crying while recovering the dead and helping the wounded, on foot or in vehicles. The soldiers are angry and those nearby are not viewing me with any degree of kindness, to say the least. I start hoofing it north away from the crowds that remain near the structures on the eastern edge of the facility, not sure just where I'm heading.

I haven't gone that far but do make the line between the airfield and Da Nang proper, when a jeep comes barreling along. As it approaches me, it's apparent an American is driving. My luck is holding for that American is my friend Captain Len Peters, the intelligence advisor to General Luong.

He pulls up beside me and stops, not recognizing me for a moment, other than being an American soldier.

"Is that you Winslow? What the fuck are you doing out here? These guys are angry, mean, in a killing mood. They've had it with Americans and blame us for this fiasco. They'll shoot your ass off if you aren't careful."

"Man, I'm glad to see you," is my reply as I jump in the rear seat. He has an ARVN soldier riding shotgun with a M-60 draped over his lap. Am I happy. Peters is looking into the mortar fire that has been reported as incoming at the north end of the base. I tell him that I heard it, that it was incoming, and that it very likely wasn't ours. Rumors that a small contingent of NVA had entered Da Nang from the Northwest were probably valid. They might be a scouting party in advance of a force large enough to take over the Air Base. I fill Peters in on the World flight that left a short time ago, along with the complete chaos that had ensued.

"One good thing though, Omar made it on the plane. The last man. I wouldn't have believed it if I hadn't seen it."

"He was sure lucky. I know he was worried that he wouldn't make it home in time to help his wife and kids."

Then Peters says, "I don't know how far you'll want to ride along with me Ed. It might be risky, and I don't have time to run you back into town."

"Don't worry my man, I'll jump out when we're on a peaceful street that's clear of the crowds."

That seemed sensible. We ride slowly along as the crowds dictate. We encounter an inordinate number of soldiers wandering, obviously without any order, or indeed presence of commanding officers. Apparently, they've all jumped ship too. And more than likely, heading in the direction of Saigon, making an exodus ahead of the NVA juggernaut.

We approach the outer limits of the city. No one is on the streets. It's eerie, and time for me to part ways with Peters and hoof it back to the pad on Tran Phu. I thank Peters and jump out saying I'll meet up with him later at the Bamboo if he makes it back before midnight.

After walking along for a short time, I suddenly think I'm in the Bamboo. It's Van Ly, walking down the street toward me.

"Van Ly, what are you doing here," I say in a low voice as we meet.

"What do you think you are doing my captain? You should not be anywhere near this part of town. It be too dangerous. They are in this neighborhood." Fear shows on her face.

"Well, I guess you could say I'm lost." I then describe the scene at the airport earlier in the day, how I had met up with Capt. Peters, then decided to leave him and walk back home.

"I think you may not make it back home tonight my captain." Then two youngish men walk out of the shadows. Black pajama clad men who are carrying AKs.

I look at them… then at her, and ask, "what the hell Van Ly, what's going on. You're not…are you?"

"Yes, my captain, I am. I be VC," and I caught a hint of a smile in her eyes.

"Ok Van Ly, we can discuss that later, but what's happening with me?"

"For now, we walk along. It be safer for you. You be shot if they see you alone walking through town."

"That's not what I mean Van Ly. I can protect myself. Am I a prisoner?"

"Yes, you be a prisoner, but I will look out for you. We can walk along with these guys to where they have a safe house and maybe we can talk. Have tea and food there."

As I walk along, I think back on my many conversations with this girl, this rather mysterious girl at times, and a realization enters my mind.

"Are you a spy for the other side Van Ly," I ask her. "Are you really a spy?"

The black pajama guy walking behind me pokes his gun in my back. I turn around and speak to him in Vietnamese. "What for? What I do wrong?"

He's surprised. He looks at his partner. Neither one speaks.

"That might not have been a good move, my Captain… speaking Vietnamese. They may start thinking. I have no control here. Not about you… not me even. Just be girl spy…not boss."

I have no idea what's happening but my focus for the day had been to arrange some kind of transport for Lien to Saigon. It still is. From there Sandy or someone can help her make it to Hong Kong where I hope at some point to join her. I'm sure Saigon is weeks off from this scene. Man, I've gotta start thinking, but good.

We walked along the street for another few minutes, then enter a narrow alley, the kind that make up the background of every Vietnamese city. Not so far in, we stop at a coffee stand in front of a non-discreet building. The men motioned to Van Ly and me that we should take a seat at the stand. One remained outside watching us and the other enters the building. Van

Ly orders tea but I request a beer which is produced without any discussion. I'm wondering what's next.

"Don't worry Captain Winslow. These are my people. Most of them are more tired of this war than you could ever be. It has been their life since they were children. For me too. My father was a VC soldier but had to 'retire' if that is the word because he lost the sight of his eye from shrapnel when I was a schoolgirl. Now he is back working as a farmer. He only needs one eye for that job. You think he wants more war? He does not care who wins. He just wants to be left alone on his farm. Just hoe rice till he dies. Not asking for so much."

I certainly have no argument with her on that subject…or her father. I just want to reach Australia with my Lien and do as her father. No war until I die.

"But you see Van Ly, I have to get back to Lien somehow and arrange for her to travel to Saigon. I must do that."

"I understand my captain. I never call you Ed before, I can do?"

I had to laugh at that one. "Of course, Van Ly. Why not? Any name will work for me. But now how about arranging my escape from these soldiers."

Before answering, the soldier who had entered the building returned and motioned us inside where we were both interrogated by a higher-ranking cadre. He was suspicious of Van Ly since it was apparent we knew each other. She tried to explain the situation. That we were acquainted from the bar scene where she had worked for over a year. Nothing more. He is skeptical and begins questioning Van Ly in more depth… rather nastily. I interrupt, in Vietnamese of course, which appears to be a repeat of my previous mistake. He looks up and says noting but motioned us to an adjoining room He then addresses Van Ly.

"You two stay here for the night. I will talk with higher headquarters, then see you in the morning."

With that he slams the door on us, and we are left alone in the dark. It's time for me to be truly worried.

The room is empty except for a mattress of sorts lying in one corner. We sit there for a spell in silence, thinking. I was beginning to fear that this was more than serious. It could be the end.

"How does it look to you Van Ly? I'm scared."

"I be too" she answered, "for I think that we are more under the control of the army from the North. Not with the local militias that I am familiar with, that I have worked with for a time. These are different people."

Earlier my intention had been to interrogate her and learn just who she was and how much info she had spread along. Now, it didn't seem to matter. We lie down next to each other for warmth and companionship. She begins telling me of her connection with the other side. It seems she's been no more than a messenger for her family and friends who happened to be with the NLF rather than the ARVN. Understandable enough.

"I am scared, and cold Captain Ed. Get closer to me. I be so cold."

I ask her to come closer and we wrap ourselves around each other. There was AK fire in the distance, and she presses closer… then the sound of an exploding grenade. We lay there in silence till all becomes quiet. Nothing from the guards nor the town outside. Her face was snuggled against my chest. I can feel her loosening and looking up at me. I lean down and kiss her. We begin cuddling, touching, and feeling each other. In short order we end up in a fierce sexual embrace. For now, she is more than my friend Van Ly. This need for primal release, I'd experienced before. It was in Tam Hiep years ago after a close call with VC members of my then girlfriends' family.

Both of us are breathless as we release our hold on each other and again lie in silence. There is no need for words. For me, one who has always related sex with love, I now don't want to leave her.

"If there is nothing from the guards, we must try to escape," she says quietly, mentioning nothing of what has happened between us.

This is too soon for me. I can think of nothing, but what has happened between us, and struggle to come around.

"I can see nothing Van Ly. What do you think is possible?"

"Let me see if I can get the guards attention. If so, and he comes in here, you must disable him somehow. We have to escape. I must go my own way and complete my mission. It be a private mission…for my husband who I haven't seen in half a year. You must somehow return to Lien and find your escape."

She rises to her feet and begins pounding on the door, yelling something in Vietnamese so fast that I'm unable to grasp the meaning. The guard eventually pokes his head inside and says to keep quiet. As he does, I grab him around the head from the side and bashed it into the wall. It knocks him out. I look outside and seeing no one else, we immediately take to our feet and run up the street.

"I must go now my captain." I can see her face in the light from the stars as she says, "Maybe I love you too, my captain. Go now…maybe we meet again some time…in many years when the war be no more. Good luck my friend."

With that she turns and trots off down the street disappearing into one of the darkest alleys. I very quickly return to the real world, realizing I'm in strange territory. I know Da Nang quite well but in no way recognize this area. Since Van Ly has gone in one direction, I take the other thinking it will be away from 'her compadres'. I know that Capt. Peters had disappeared somewhere in this area and had hope that I might luck out and run back into him. The warmth and sexual sensitivities of Van Ly remain in my brain. But I must transition to Lien and the US Consulate immediately if there is to be a successful conclusion to this night, or in fact this life.

Luck is not with me this early morning before darkness leads to the lightness. I wander down numerous streets and alleys trying to orient myself for I know Da Nang, or so I think. From the stars I could see I have been walking west which is not in the right direction. I stop for a moment to think when two men walk out of the shadows. They are wearing pith helmets indicating NVA. ARVN wear American helmets or soft caps or Aussie bush hats. One of them said "Halt" in Vietnamese.

I do so and asked him in his language, "who are you? What do you want with me?"

He answers in no uncertain terms that he is the one asking the questions.

"You are my prisoner. I am going to take you to my sergeant."

I considered running but thought better of that option, thinking a bullet in the back would not help Lien make it to Australia, not to mention myself.

CHAPTER 26:

US CONSULATE,
DA NANG

JAKE BARNS AND ARTHUR EVEREST ARE STANDING IN front of the US Consulate on the Han River in Da Nang along with Deputy Consul General Wales Signor. It's the day of the last World Airways flight from Da Nang. Captain Edward Winslow is nowhere in sight. The Bamboo Bar down the street is closed. The crowd is building. A large barge is tied to the pier across from the consulate for the purpose of evacuating refugees to the armada of US Navy boats and ships that are anchored some distance offshore. A white man is walking towards them. It's Emerson Fitz.

"So what's happening Soldier Boys? Doesn't look good, does it?"

"Fuck you Fitz. You some kind of traitor or something?" It's Art Everest, the Navy Seal.

"Never happen GI. I'm just one of your normal, intelligent Americans that can think for himself. Ten years of US bombing and this place is going down the tubes. And that's why. I've been working with the people here for eight years. Seen it all just about and you know what? A little common sense and there could have been a very different ending. Too bad. Too bad for all of us. There will be no winners when this comes around."

"Just what we need, a bleeding-heart liberal," is the Seal's reply.

There's silence for a moment. Apparently, no one wants to dig farther into this. It's not the time.

Signor speaks up. "The issue at the moment is how to help all of these people? How the hell are we going to get out of here. I for one don't look forward to being a POW, if that's what's they call a civilian in these circumstances," said Signor.

Then Barns pipes in with "don't worry Signor, my chopper is going to show up here at some point and I intend to run a shuttle to the Marble Mountain strip where at least one C-47 will be flying to Saigon."

"The thing is" says Signor, "I can't leave till orders come in to abandon the consulate. They want me to hang on until all of our employees and their families that wish to leave the country are on a plane, or a barge to one of the ships offshore. I can't locate most of them. And I have no idea at all how many want to leave. And more to the point, I don't know how many are involved with the opposition. In plain English, how many are VC and been working against our ass for their term of employment. Fuck me."

"Don't let it get to you Wales," says Barns. "This is all going to play out, with or without us. Nothing to worry about."

General Luong approaches the American soldiers. He is flustered, disheveled.

"Major Barns," states the General. "Where is your helicopter? I was depending on it for my escape to Saigon. My orders were to leave yesterday, however I stayed to do what I could for the soldiers under my command. But now I am finished. I must save myself and get to my family in Saigon."

Wales immediately takes General Luong under his arm and herds him into the consulate where he'll be safe from the crowd. Many of the ARVN

soldiers are unnerved, scared and mad as hell at their officers who have abandoned them in the field. They would have no way of knowing that General
Luong was of the opposite type.

Barns is concerned for Lien. "If Winslow doesn't show I need to find
Lien. She needs a ride out of here and I expect to help. Banks and my copilot
should have the Huey flying soon and will be here shortly."

Barns and Everest are left thinking by themselves while scanning the
crowds. They both see Lien approaching. She's upset, flustered.

"Have you seen Captain Winslow? I cannot find, " she implores them.

Barns speaks to her as she approaches. " Lien, you must stay with me
until we see how this scene unfolds. There is still time for Captain Winslow
to make it back here unless he has made the World Airways flight that left
some hours ago. If he isn't on it, he should be back here soon unless he's met
trouble at the airport."

"No, he would not go, he would not leave me, I know that for sure," as
she tears up.

Jake Barns takes her into his arms, comforting her with assurances
that her man will be ok.

Wales Signor has returned to the pier and is helping load civilians on
the barge with the help of the other American officers. Suddenly a shot ring
outs. A group of ARVN soldiers are breaking in ahead of the civilians and one
of them has shot a woman who looked to have been with her children. The
bodies of two kids that have been trampled by these soldiers still lay beneath
their feet, this apparently being irrelevant to them.

"I'll shoot that filthy son of a bitch," yells Lt. Everest who then pulls his
pistol and shoots the offender in the head. The soldier falls into the river, not
moving. No one cares or gives a damn. Then Everest walks over to the other
ARVN and lines them all out. They listen, though perhaps not understanding
his exact words. His anger is evident, as is the result. In the course of this
melee the raft has drifted some distance from the pier with more refugees

falling into the river. As it's pulled back, more are crushed when it slams into the pier once again. Signor is trying to maintain some semblance of order without having much or any success. He is horrified by what was happening.

"Step back," cries Everest. "I'll take charge of this."

He pulls his pistol and begins firing in the air. Nothing happens. No one stops, or even seems to notice. After all, they'd been hearing gunfire all their lives. More women and children are boarding, the last to make it on board, before the tug begins to pull it away from the pier. The ARVN who are dead set on escaping have reattached a line. A few to their horror have fallen into the water between the pier and the barge and are crushed as it once again pushes against the pier. Finally, this old boat breaks free and the tug begins forcing it down the river towards the Bay of Da Nang. Everest sees another barge tied up next to the Bamboo that's also surrounded by a large crowd with screaming and gunfire going on.

"Listen Barns, I'm going to walk to the next barge and see if I can be of any help."

Then Lien comes over and says, 'I can't find Van Ly. She has disappeared. She is my friend and would tell me and I am worried about her."

Barns has been pursuing Van Ly for some time, to no avail. but he knows her fairly well. "I think Van Ly is caught in the middle, like most of the people in this country. Who knows? She could be anywhere. Is anyone running the Bamboo, Lien ?

"No, no, It be closed. No customers and no workers. Bamboo fini."

"Just like this country," mumbles Barns, to no one in particular.

Arthur Everest, a navy Seal to the end finally makes it to the barge by the Bamboo where a similar scene is unfolding. ARVN Marines and Infantry are once again crowding aboard the barge with no regard for the civilians attempting the same movement. The Viet troops are shooting the civilians in their mad rush to escape, not even knowing this barge's destination. Everest fires his pistol in the air once more, attempting to gain their attention. Some of them hesitate and look his way but a couple of the Marines pay no heed while continuing to shoot civilians in their way, who fall into the river between the barge and the pier. Everest does not hesitate. He shoots both of the offending soldiers who also drop into the river. The other native soldiers stand back as he approaches them with the pistol in his hand. He takes charge and organizes an orderly departure, after all who will fit are on board.

Emerson Fitz, Barns, Everest and Signor are once again standing on the street in front of the consulate, trying to decide their next move. Lien is still with them. Emerson is trying to calm her down, telling her that Winslow will somehow show up. Or if not, he'll make his way to Saigon on his own. Either way she must leave, however it's possible at this point.

"Where the hell is Peters," exclaims Everest. "He should be here. He's probably got some weird bullshit going on and is stuck somewhere. Intelligence people… they'll fuck anything up."

Signor tells them he has to get back inside the consulate building and help wrapping up visas for his employees and their families. Anyone who has been working with the Americans can be in jeopardy. They all remember the example set in Hue during the Tet Offensive of '68. It wasn't a pretty scene. Supposedly as many as two thousand suspected collaborators with the Americans were killed in cold blood. Executed. There is no way of knowing whether the NVA will follow that same pattern or not.

"I'm hoping this will be a different scene," says Signor to no one in particular. "The scent of victory is in the air, and I don't believe the desire for revenge will be that important."

"Let's hope not," says Everest, "but I don't trust any of the bastards. The main rule of warfare is 'trust no one'. That's mine too. I made it up, and so far it's worked for me."

Suddenly the sound of Huey…then it becomes visible, flying up the river towards the consulate.

"Finally," Barns says to himself, " I thought they'd never get here."

The Huey circles and slowly sets down at the rear of the consulate building away from the crowds on the street who'd likely over run it and prevent any evacuations. The Americans enter the consulate grounds with the exception of Everest who stands guard at the gate. Barn's Vietnamese copilot is flying, and Banks is manning the M-60 on the right side. The pilot remains at the controls. He's flying from the right seat so Barns will be able to quickly take his regular position as aircraft commander on the left. Banks jumps out as the aircraft idles and runs over to talk with Barns.

"What's up here Major? Who are we taking, and where are we going? We just left Marble Mountain and there was still one C-47 and a C-46 on the ground ready to take off for Saigon whenever they take on a load of passengers. There were a couple of CIA Porters there also. Who knows what they're up to?"

At that moment Signor runs up to Barns.

"Do you think you could make a couple of trips to Marble Mountain. The Embassy in Saigon has a C-46 on standby for whoever we feel is at the most risk from our pool of employees and their families. What about it Barns?"

"Can do, let me get strapped in, then load it up. I'm sure we can make a least a couple of runs. If there ends up being no air transport out of the Marble Mountain airfield there should be some local boats making it out to sea from My Khe beach where they'll be able to transfer to US Navy ships on station for that purpose. Let's get going."

Signor runs inside the consulate building and begins herding the consulate employees that he wants excavated first. The Vietnamese always have extended families, so the crowd has no limits. They are able to pack fifteen. mostly women and kids inside. Barns corkscrewed up and over the building then down the river. The airfield is less than ten minutes away. In short order he's back for another load. Everest has found someone to guard the front entrance and is talking to Signor as the Huey drops back in. Lien is with them.

"I cannot leave without my captain," she tells Everest while crying her eyes out. "He would never leave me. Something must have happened."

"Lien," implores Everest, "you must leave now. I will do my best to find your man. You must get to Saigon while you can. When you arrive, check in at the Kangaroo Bar where you can find a man named John Sanderson. He is with the Australian Army, and he will help you. Stay in touch with him. Either Barns or I will be by there one way or the other and hopefully Captain Winslow as well. We will not abandon him in the field. Do not worry."

With that he loads Lien in with the next round of refugees from the consulate employee pool. Once again Barns spirals up and slips the old Huey down the river towards Marble Mountain which remains visible in the distance. The mountain, not the airfield. He'd been ordered when he dropped off the first load, to have Signor on board next time. The C-46 waiting on the ramp is being held for the diplomat. He's the last important refugee as far as the US government is concerned. Consequently, Barns knew that they'd hold for one more trip. He dropped his passengers off assuring Lien that she will find space on board, then once again returns to the Consulate.

Lt. Everest has a group waiting for this last trip out. General Luong is among them. He had been hesitant, knowing that he has to go but still waiting, holding back.

"It's now or never General," states Everest. "If you miss, you'll have the rest of your life to regret it.

General Luong salutes the captain, turns on his heel and walks to the helicopter, never looking back. Just then Captain Peters showed up being driven in an ARVN jeep. He quickly relays the information that he had seen Captain Winslow but had left him to make his way back here.

"No chance of that now," says Everest. "He'll have to find some other solution,"

Everest runs over to relay this important information to Barns who has remained at the controls of his idling aircraft. As he walks back Barns lifts off…without Signor, his intended passenger.

Barns had told Peters that since he had the general on board for the flight to Saigon that he is confident he will be able to manage one more shuttle for the Assistant Consul General.

"What about you Peters," declares Everest. "You staying?" as he grinned.

"My ass is out of here with Signor. I'm no damn fool. After leaving Winslow we drove west till those green pith helmets were actually visible. You get it…NVA troops. We U turned immediately and drove like hell back here. This place isn't holding for more than a day or so more. You'd better move your ass too."

"I'm a navy man, a Seal. I'll swim to Saigon if I have to, before I'll leave with my tail between my legs on a fucking Army helicopter. Don't worry about me. I'm still thinking."

"Be a fucking idiot if you want, but I'm leaving with Signor and Barns on that Huey, US Army or not."

Then, Barns is back. Everest runs over after the chopper spools down to see if this is it.

"The last flight from here," said Barns. "I'll tell you that. Signor has to be on this flight and that plane is leaving Marble Mountain soon as he boards. They were royally pissed off when he didn't show on the last flight."

Signor then leaves the consulate with the last of his work force and their families. They are carrying a few boxes of papers and he has the flag that has flown above the building since 1964, draped unceremoniously over his shoulder."

"Get on with them" Everest tells Peters. "I'm sticking around for a bit. Still got some loose ends to take care of."

"Good luck my man." They shook hands then Peters turns and runs for the Huey as it's lifting off. He makes the skid just in time.

After landing at the airfield, they can see the C-46 has its engines idling. Barns too is having second thoughts."

"Let's go," said Peters. Banks jumped from the gunner's position after the other passengers have disembarked.

"We on this flight Major Barns?" was Banks inquiry.

"Jump on Banks, I'll be seeing you in Saigon."

"That's no good Major. Let's go."

"Climb aboard Banks, that's an order. I'll be seeing you at the chopper pad at Tan Son Nhut. Have no fear."

Banks clambers aboard the old C- 46 as it began to move. He can see a truckload of ARVN screeching to a halt just by the aircraft's tail. They jump from the truck and run for the plane. Banks had managed to close the door, but some barge forward and jump up on the tail. Barns is trying to pull them off.

"Do you fucking idiots think you can ride to Saigon on the wings? Let go, get the hell off, you'll crack up the plane."

He eventually clears the tail, and the plane slowly picks up speed. It's grossly overloaded. Finally, as it nears the end of the runway, the old machine struggles into the air, staying in ground effect till it picks up enough speed to begin a shallow climb. It veers to the left for it could never clear the mountain, then continues climbing to a safe altitude over the South China Sea.

Barns stands there, watching until it disappears from sight. One of the ARVN soldiers that he had pulled to the ground has stayed. He is standing beside him on the ramp.

"Is that it Major? The final exodus of the great United States"

Barns is surprised at the good English used by an ARVN private.

"I can think too, not just speak" the soldier says.

"Yes, I see," said Barns. "What's your name soldier?"

"Private Singh. I know who you are Major Barns. Before I have ridden on your helicopter for more than one mission. You OK pilot."

Barns just nods. Both are silent for a short period. Then Singh discloses his deep thoughts. "We all knew it deep down. You people always thought you were better than us. That you were smarter than us. That we couldn't run our own country. You were bigger than us. How big now Major? When you all run away. Like the cowards you are. Now we must face the NVA alone."

"Well, they're your people," said Barns. "I've been told by your country-man more than once that they'd just as soon see them win. Go for it private."

The ARVN looks up at him but before he can speak Barns continues.

"Forget what I've said, Private Singh. You are right. We failed. We have failed you and your country, and we have failed ourselves, and it began many years ago. So many mistakes… but now this is where we are, this is where it ends. So, good luck to you Private Singh. I must be moving on."

Barns walks away towards the Air America section on the ramp where a pilot of the remaining CIA Porter is sitting on a bench. It's the faithful Lee Mullins.

"What's up old friend? You're not staying here I presume," said Barns.

"No, but I'd like to," said Mullins, 'there's nowhere else in the world for me to go."

"There's always time for a new beginning Lee. Just hold your head up, and get with it."

"Perhaps I've told you Barns, but it's ten years for me in old Indochina. Three in Laos, six here and one in Cambodia. I'm in Cambodia as far as anyone knows at the moment. This is just a quick secret trip. Who knows why? Maybe collecting an opium debt. Never met my passenger before, and don't give much of a damn any how. What about you Barns? You'd better get a move on."

"I'd like to but I'm waiting for morning to see if a friend shows up. You know Ed Winslow, don't you?"

"Sure. Gave him a ride to Saigon and back a couple of times. What's up?"

"He should have been on that C-46 that just left, and I should have been with him. Not sure what the hell has happened. Just waiting till tomorrow and taking it from there."

"I'd hang around till morning too if I could. Maybe help you guys out, but my passenger has to be in Phnom Penh by midnight. That place is close to going to hell in a handbasket to, faster than Saigon."

Yea, it's too bad," said Barns, "but it had to happen. Too many fuck ups all around. A misbegotten venture gone bad. So let's pack up and begin anew. That's got a certain ring to it."

"I can do it," said Mullens, "I have to, but I don't want to. It's a fucking ball breaker."

"Well, good luck Lee. Think I'll find a place to sack out here till morning. I'd like to look up a girl I know at the Bamboo, but the streets are not going to be safe tonight. That is a certainty."

Just up the beach towards Monkey Mountain at My Khe a lone American is looking out at the flotilla that's visible on the moonlit horizon. It's the Navy Seal, Lt. Arthur Everest. Some ARVN also stand there, watching him.

"It's all finished," he says to not one of them in particular. Then he strips off his uniform and runs into the surf. Lt. Everest disappears in the distance, swimming eastward towards the rising moon, and the ships of the US Navy.

CHAPTER 27:

_____

SAIGON - 1975

A RENAULT TAXI PULLS UP IN FRONT OF THE AMERICAN
Embassy in Saigon. Two passengers, a man and a woman depart. They have
no luggage. The man is Wales Signor, Assistant US Consul General from the
US Consulate in Da Nang. The woman is Lien, wife of his good friend US
Army Captain Edward Winslow. They remain talking in front of the embassy
as the cab drives off.

"Lien," Signor tells her, "Why don't you come inside with me, and I'll
figure something out. Right now I must report to the Ambassador, immediately. Afterwards I might be able to leave. Why not try?"

"No, no Mr. Wales, my husband tells me to report to the Kangaroo
Bar and see John Sanderson of the Australian Army. I know. It be only a few
blocks. I will walk there now. If there be trouble, I will let you know, and
thank you for your help."

"Don't worry about Captain Winslow. I know him. He will be here…
maybe tomorrow."

Signor leaves her with the embassy phone number, and she walks down the street turning by the Notre Dame Cathedral, then down Tu Do St. She is not at all sure Winslow will make it.

John Sanderson is in the Kangaroo talking with Tot, the owner.

"Doesn't look good Tot. Bad word from Da Nang. Maybe VC win."

"For sure" she says. "Why not? Sometime American go home, Aussie go home. All foreigners go home, Vietnam stay. VC win."

Sandy stops and thinks for a moment. "Have you always thought that, Tot?"

"For sure. I know. Have friends other side. You want more beer, Sandy?"

"For sure… but tell me Tot, have you always thought, or should I say known, it would end this way? And what about you?"

"Always know. I be ok. Have friends."

No wonder we're losing the fucking thing Sandy is thinking to himself. Then Khanh joins him. She's been talking with a customer who has left. She's his favorite girl…and the smartest.

"Sandy, I want go Australia. Tot can stay with VC and NVA. When they take over from the South, they will run things. We from the South will have hard time. You take me with you, ok Sandy?"

"Never know my friend Khanh. Maybe can do, may cannot do." Sandy was one who had a number of girlfriends and 'who can know'?

Then Lien enters the bar and joins them. Sandy recognizes her.

"Lien, how did you get here? I had word that the last plane from Marble Mountain has made it in."

"Yes," she replies, "and I was on it. My friends make me leave before Captain Winslow comes back, so I come here and wait for him. That what he ask me to do."

Before Sandy can reply, Sgt. Omar walks in. "Sandy, how you be?" he yells in a voice that is normal for him.

He waves Omar over for a beer and continues with Lien. "Don't worry about your man Winslow my girl. He'll show up here. There's no doubt about that."

Eventually even Wales Signor shows up checking on Lien. The conversation runs hot and cold. Was the whole country disintegrating? Would it end with Da Nang? Would Winslow make it down tomorrow? Would some sort of accommodation be made with the North to end it all here and now? But whatever happens the general consensus was that it was time. Time to wrap it up.

"I'm eight years tired," says Omar. "It time to be home."

CHAPTER 28:

NVA CAMP -

SGT CHANH

SERGEANT CHANH AND HIS MEN HAVE SET UP CAMP FOR the night. They've reached the ridge just west of the airport and are sitting around the fire, talking. Their mood has improved. They can see the end, and it's not living forever in the jungle, getting nowhere. The younger soldiers are wondering if any of the local girls will be available when they enter Da Nang, or any of the pleasures they've heard of from movies and magazines.

"Let's get all their food and whiskey when we find their living quarters," said Private Cong. "I know our meals have improved lately, but for too long we have eaten rice and nuoc mam"

"Let's arrive safely, all of us," said Sgt. Chanh, "before we begin dividing up the spoils of war. I can say nothing will be worth it...at least for myself. Too many years have gone by. I miss what could have been my life".

"Don't worry Sergeant," said Corporal Huu, "you will return to Thai Nguyen and your one true love and live happily ever after, just like in the stories."

Chanh thought about that but could not be a believer. Not after all that he'd seen. But no need to put the younger soldiers in the dumps.

"Who knows" said Chanh, "Perhaps all of those local beauties are waiting to be saved by you valiant soldiers from the North. Who can know?"

Captain Bao came over to their section of the compound to check on readiness for movements into Da Nang in the morning. The plan is to move on Da Nang…first through the air base. The main force is still somewhere in the vicinity of Hai Van Pass, either side or on top. Captain Bao's unit is being used more as a forward observer, to feel out the area regarding both remaining ARVN, as well as the local population. Soldiers from the North know nothing of the southern society.

Early the next morning Sgt. Chanh and his troops leave early. By sunup they are inside the air base fence and holed up in one of the old US Airforce revetments. In this area all is peaceful. There are no soldiers or air force personnel in sight. Eventually the platoon makes its way to a warehouse that appears be used for the storage of PX supplies and commodities. The soldiers from the farms of the countryside of northern Vietnam have no idea what all of these 'things' are. Most have never heard of, much less seen, televisions or refrigerators, these massive tape recorders and stereos. These material things. Shelves of whiskey and wines and cigarettes are the only commodities of real interest to the bo dai, these country boys from the North.

"Corporal Huu," said Sgt.Chanh, "keep order among these troops. Try and limit any hoarding of supplies that are found here. I have to check back with Captain Bao and see what further orders might be. As you can see there is no one here. Where have all the enemies gone?

Sargent Chanh has located Captain Bao and they are discussing their options. Word still has not reached them on the larger occupying force that has been traveling down Route #1 from Hue. It looks as if Da Nang can be taken without much of a battle. Perhaps less. The two old soldiers pour themselves tea and sit down for a talk. They are not old men, but this war has gotten old for them. Something like a third of their lives. Chanh is lying back in his hammock while Captain Bao settles into a reclining seat made from filled sandbags left over from the Americans.

"You know I try Captain Bao, but I can no longer be a believer."

"Believer in what Chanh?"

"The system of my country. The system of the Party that is supposed to be everything. Look around us here, our troops. They are all poor boys from the country. The Party big shots protect their sons. They live better than us."

"You'd best be careful on who you talk to Chanh," said Captain Bao. "Do not let the political cadre hear this. It would not go well for you."

"You know what Captain, I would like to just say 'fuck you' to all of them. It's way too much for me. I want a simple life on the farm with the woman that I love. Let them all stay in the city, far and away from me."

"I think it is this war Sgt. Chanh. Whatever you think about the Party and its government, it has led us to victory. That is a sure thing now."

"It is but look at us. Our youth is gone."

"Cheer up Chanh. We've been too long in this war. Things will get better when you return to the fields. Who knows, you might end up moving to Hanoi and joining the Party," said Bao as he smiles at Chanh.

They both lie back and shut their eyes, taking a needed break from the war… and their men.

Private Lahn, a boy of eighteen who is new to the army walks over to awaken both of his senior cadre who have fallen into a deep snooze.

"Sgt. Chanh, Captain Bao, quickly you must come,"

The two old soldiers come to not realizing that they've slept for some time.

"What is it Private Lahn? What's wrong," as Chanh responds.

"No, no, it is not trouble. We have put together with the rest of the company a feast made from all the supplies that the puppet troops have left behind."

The two NCOs follow the private towards the row of revetments, finally stopping at one that is fully occupied.

Tables have been set up and are heaped with food, drink. A large group of bo doi from their units have gathered for what appears to be a feast, a real feast, not something from their camps with wild vegetables from the jungle and stewed rats from overgrown fields of grain.

Private Lahn motions them over to the head of one of the tables where they are given seats of honor. The other solders do not take notice.

"Have you noticed Captain Bao, how most of the faces of the celebrants are young. They don't even know why they are celebrating. There are old faces here, but not many like ours. We've seen too much to celebrate. After so much death and destruction… why bother."

Laughter and toasts ring all around cheered on by the beer and wine and whiskey that has been rescued from the abandoned US PX.

The feasting goes into the afternoon, then the men rest, to sleep it off before the evening's march.

A courier approaches Captain Bao. His message is to wait till morning when a push will begin. The high command wants to reassess then and be sure that Da Nang is secured and that the final offensive can recommence.

Chanh and Bao return to their camp on the outskirts of the airfield. Captain Bao leaves his sergeant in command of his troops and travels back farther in the rear to consult with his superiors. One by one or in twos the men return, and sack out early, over done by the food and drink, the likes of which many of them have never seen.

Then a soldier runs up with a message. There is a prisoner, an American.

A group of bo doi enter the camp, dragging along an American whose arms are tightly bound behind him.

"Guess what sergeant, he speaks our language."

CHAPTER 29:

WINSLOW
CAPTURED

THEY TIED MY HANDS BEHIND MY BACK, MUCH TIGHTER than necessary, then began marching me back from the way I'd come. It went slowly. I still had not shaken off my exquisite sexual experience with Van Ly, who I might not ever see again. It entered my mind that I might not see any of them again. I had no idea where they were taking me, and they obviously did not know the way, wherever the way was. It took hours, and when dawn broke, they really slowed down, apparently unsure of the conditions and security of Da Nang from the perspective of the NVA.

A few people were beginning to appear on the streets. We walked by a pho stand where the pot was boiling, so stopped for directions. The old woman was excited to see the northern soldiers with a prisoner no less and offered us all a bowl as well as a spot to lie back and rest. I nodded off and wasn't awakened till mid-morning. One soldier was sleeping, but the other remained on guard, watching.

"Hey soldier," I asked him in his language, "where are we going?"

He eyed me suspiciously, unsure if he ought to even be speaking to an American, as strange an animal as he had ever seen. He didn't answer right off so I initiated a conversation with the old woman who was operating the pho stand and eventually worked him into it. He began warming up,"

"Why are you here?" he asked me. "All Americans go from Vietnam we are told."

This turned into a conversation that could be called friendly. The other soldier awakened and eventually joined us after a glass of tea that was offered by the old woman. From what I understood they were trying to locate their camp which from what I was able to gather from them was on the west side of the airfield, a countryside that was still quite wild. It was beyond the outskirts of Da Nang proper. By late afternoon we had the airport in sight, but they wanted to stay in the shadows of the street until darkness fell.

As we neared their destination some other soldiers met up with us, then joined our little group. They were less friendly and began pushing me around. I pushed back and one of them gave me a swat on the back of the head. I lined him out in Vietnamese. He jumped back, completely unexpecting that.

"So you smart American. We can show you how smart we are too. Just about then another older NVA soldier appeared, and he yelled at the offending bo doi who turned and left me with my original captors who were under his command.

"Sergeant Chanh, we have captured this foreign soldier last night in the northern part of Da Nang and have just arrived here in camp. We had to be careful traveling through the city with our prisoner. We have never been in such a large city before. Even knowing their language, I thought it best to remain silent for the moment.

"Why are you here, American?" said this Sergeant Chanh to me.

I explained my situation to him, saying that there was no need to hold me captive. They could just let me go and I would continue to Saigon and leave Vietnam forever.

He smiled at me saying, "are you crazy. Why should I release you? You are a prisoner of the victorious army of North Vietnam."

In my favor he then ordered his men to untie me.

"Where do you think he can go Private Huu? You men continue on with your duties. I will have a long talk with this late staying American soldier."

The bo dai grudgingly return to their preparations for tomorrows operation. They don't approve of the hospitality shown to the enemy soldier. Sgt Chanh pours tea for us both and points me towards a seat. We sit here staring at each other for a few minutes, then I think I'd better try for a positive conversation before he begins accusations, but he beats me to it.

"Name, rank and serial number soldier?" And that was it, so I give him all three which doesn't seem to interest him.

"How does it happen that you know my language?" he asks me.

"I first came to Vietnam over ten years ago," I told Sgt. Chanh. "During that time I had occasion to work with Vietnamese soldiers and I developed an interest in the language. It obviously was also helpful for the work I was doing. This was before the US Marines landed on Red Beach in March of 1965. I'd been in country for a year by then and eventually picked it up. Before returning two years ago I attended a short course at Lackland Air Force base in Texas. And I have a Vietnamese wife."

"Too much information for me Captain Winslow. You have learned it well. Where do we go with it now? What is on your mind?"

This took some thinking on my part. If at all possible, I wanted to avoid the traditional prisoner of war routine. Hell, I could be here for years. I thought there might be a way to personalize our relationship.

"How long have you been in the army Sgt. Chanh? Where are you from in Vietnam? You must be tired from this war."

"Tired, yes, I am very tired. I am tired of your country coming to Vietnam and causing all this death and destruction. Why come here? Why not stay home?"

"I can understand your feelings Sargent. Over the years I have asked myself the same questions. But that is all in the past. Now I would like to go home. I do not believe in this war any longer. I have not for a long time. I came back because I loved the country and wanted to see how this would end."

"End. It could end for you very soon….forever. Some more bad luck and the same for me."

"And for me, I fell in love with a woman from your country and married her. We hope to leave very soon and live in Australia."

"Australia. Why do you want to live in Australia? Your country is not good for you after fighting this great war in Vietnam?"

This was getting tricky. I in no way wanted to come across as some kind of traitor but in this case speaking my mind truthfully might be helpful. Establishing more of a relationship with this sergeant who appeared as disillusioned as myself might get me out of here.

"I think my country and myself both made a big mistake here in Vietnam. Sometimes in America we can be ignorant people, and for this war here in this country we were. For myself I want to get away…far away. Lien, that is my wife's name, and I want to have a fresh start and a new life as far away from America as we can go. That is Australia."

"I am very different than you, but in some ways alike. I am no communist. I do not belong to the party. Everything is not so good with us either. I want none of it. I want to hide. Maybe I want to hide from the world. Just live with the woman I love in the north. I hope it is more than a dream. If I think back, I never wanted to leave my village, but your country took care of that."

There wasn't much that I could say, other than I agreed with him and that I felt the same way myself in my own position. Then a higher-ranking officer came into the picture. He looked me up and down and said nothing, to me or to Sgt. Chanh.

Sgt. Chanh filled in the officer who turned out to be a Captain Bao, his superior officer.

He eventually questioned me in great detail much as had Sgt. Chanh. More tea was ordered and what seemed like hours went by as the three of us carried on a strange and mixed conversation, or perhaps from their position an interrogation.

I was exhausted by the end of the interrogation, and conversations with my captors, and welcomed the end when they gave me a cot to sleep on, with a guard of course.

I awakened to silence. It is just beginning to get light. Sgt. Chanh is gathering together his few belongings. The company is tucked in. Even the guards are dozing. Others are sleeping soundly in their hammocks. Chanh was up with tea brewed and he beckoned me over to the bench that served as a table. He said nothing but began to write a note to Captain Bao. I'm able to read it over his shoulder.

Dear Captain Bao…I am going home. I'm finished with the Army. I've been a soldier for too long. My war is over. Please cover for me as long as you can and look out for the men. Good Luck my friend…Sgt Chanh

Just then Huu walks up. Apparently, he's been away from the camp earlier this morning and has captured ARVN jeep.

"Sgt. Chanh, you wouldn't believe this. There is no evidence of the Army of the Republic of Viet Nam. It has disappeared into the darkness. Strange jeeps are driving through the streets of Da Nang. Except for the remnants of the reported mob along the river, Da Nang is quiet. Many ARVN remain behind, in partial uniform or civilian clothes. No arms are evident. People are at the sidewalk stalls having coffee and morning pho. The flag of the old South Viet Nam is nowhere to be seen. Buddhist banners and our flag are hung in front of many houses along the streets"

"But do you know anything of what might have happened in the city yesterday, Private Huu?"

"Things appear to be peaceful." replied Huu. "Apparently the town was captured by two Russian duce and a halfs which were seen heading for the center of town. Inside are men, along with some women from the local guerrilla forces. They were flying the flag of the National Liberation Front and I was told not a shot was fired."

"That is unbelievable," said Chanh.

I was thinking the same thing, but more than ever wondering what they were going to do with me. Then Chanh looks back at me.

"It looks like, Captain Winslow, that I will have to send you to security forces in the rear. It's too late for both of us now. My men would like to shoot you, so it is for your own good. They are young and green and anxious to kill the enemy. You are a prime suspect for they expected only troops of the puppet government."

I was silent for a moment then said "Sgt. Chanh, I think we both understand each other. We both want to leave this war and return to a normal life. It's been too long and in many ways for nothing. Would it be impossible for you to let me return to my own people?"

He looked at me then said to Corporal Huu. "Take this man to the security forces. Tell them if anything happens to him, they will be court martialed. Make that clear."

"Sure thing Sergeant," said Huu as he began to take charge of me.

Then Sargent Chanh turns back towards us and says, "Huu, wait a minute. On second thought, take him to the outskirts of camp and drive him in the jeep to the other end of the airfield…and turn him loose."

"Have you gone crazy Sergeant? Why? What if the higher ups find out?" asked Huu.

"You tell them that the prisoner was with me the last time you saw us. Tell them you know nothing."

And this is how my status as a POW ends. Huu is able to drive me to the southern portion of the airfield where he releases me. I thank him, bid him good luck and start hoofing it down a back road south as the sun is rising in the east. I was thinking that at the same time Sergeant Chanh was in the same position as myself. Only he was heading north, alone and hopefully free.

I walk for some time and eventually make it past Marble Mountain, which is visible to my east, but some distance away.

The elation of being free is over whelming however I have no idea what to expect. Other than a few farmers tending to the fields, I can see no other humans. Quite frankly fear is entering my persona. In a nutshell, I'm scared like hell.

Then suddenly I hear the wop...wop...wop of a helicopter. I can see the small form in the distance along the southern edge of Marble Mountain. As it comes closer, I can see that it's the same old Huey with the insignia of the 1st Cav on its nose. In short order it swoops down and lands in the road directly in front of me. I run for the machine and jump aboard. The pilot turns and smiles at me. It's Jake Barns. I've never been so glad to see someone in my life. He points out a helmet that's plugged to the intercom and I put it on.

"Never thought you'd see me again, did you, you fuckhead. What in hell were you thinking?"

I answer him briefly considering the noise of the chopper as we lift off and head south.

We are able to fuel up in Qui Nhon ahead of the NVA juggernaut and make the rest of the way to Saigon by fueling at isolated outposts that Barns is familiar with. That my luck held to this extent is unbelievable. It is due to the goodness of an NVA soldier that I had known for just a brief time, a time I will never forget, a soldier whose face will be stamped forever in my memory.

CHAPTER 30:

HANOI -
THE PRESENT

IT WAS LATE AND GETTING LATER AT THE METROPOLE BAR, but for myself none of it mattered. Wales had meetings first thing in the morning at the Embassy and Mai checked in at her day job with Morrison Knudson early, so both were looking to get going. We were the only customers left.

"Let's get at it boys. Morning's coming and I need my beauty sleep." It's Mai, and she means it.

"I don't know Wales, but maybe I should make a run to Da Nang before leaving," I mention, "just for the hell of it."

He replied with, "I've got to go down there and check in with my source for news of central Viet Nam that can be useful for us at the Embassy. Come along. There's a flight tomorrow at one or so. Get on it and I'll meet you at the airport. Will that solve your problem?"

Well, it would solve my tomorrow problem. We all three then packed it in for the night.

I had taken my seat on the Vietnam Airlines flight to Da Nang hoping that Wales was going to show up. The flight looked full. Then I notice him walking back towards the tail of the plane where I'm sitting.

"Come up front with me Ed, I OKed it with the girls. You don't expect an ambassador to ride back here with the peons, do you?"

I smiled to myself at that, knowing that he was only half joking, and rose to join him up front thinking that it affects them all in the end.

After being served a glass of wine I enquired about his source. "Don't we have a consulate in Da Nang?"

"Hell no. You think there's a war going on?"

Always the funny guy, Wales Signor. "No, I don't believe so, but why the hell wouldn't they? Da Nang is the geographic center of the Country, and the third largest city, so why not?"

"No funding. And no need. Nothing going on there of any interest presently. When things pick up, maybe."

"Then who the hell are you dealing with, Van Ly, if she's still alive and living in Da Nang?"

Then he really began laughing like hell and couldn't or wouldn't stop. When he did, "You don't know do you?"

"What the fuck man, come out and say it. I have no Idea."

"Van Ly is the mayor of Da Nang."

This bowls me over. I am speechless. From where we all were in those last days, I'd have thought it was a miracle if she had just survived. It turned out that she'd been on that job for the last two years and was doing well at it.

"Do you see much of her," I asked. "Is she married?"

"She was always married. He was the NLF cadre that headed the committee which ran the shadow government of Da Nang back when we were there."

I was silent for a spell thinking about my last moments with Van Ly… after our time of intimacy. A memory that's never left me over my long life with Lien.

"I think her husband has taken ill," said Wales. "I've never met him, but I see her on occasion though she is not my contact down there. Obviously. She could hardly be a secure line of information for the US, do you think?"

I told him I would probably agree with him though I really didn't give a damn one way or the other.

"No, my contact in Da Nang is our old friend Emerson Fitz. He's back on the job working out of the very office he used back in the day. You'd never believe it…and he's just as touchy. The US is the cause of all the problems here."

I was thinking I'd probably agree with old Fitz, but let it go. Why bother at this point. There's plenty of blame to go full circle. Every faction fucked up.

"Is he working for our government?" I asked.

"No, hell no. He's working for an NGO called Rebuild Vietnam. It was founded by a wealthy Vietnamese woman from back in the States. A good outfit too. You'll see. Fitz talks a tough game but he's a commonsense person."

"He always was" I put in, "but it was pissed off common sense."

"Oddly enough," said Wales. "Fitz, Van Ly and I make a good team. We're doing a lot of good there."

The pilot intrudes, saying they are on final approach, so we belted up as he brought the Airbus in for a smooth landing. The strip is so long we could have made two.

Da Nang is different but still recognizable. Wider streets with new buildings and a good coat of paint mostly. We caught a cab and weaved through the traffic down towards the river. I was able to catch a quick view of our old love nest as we passed through Tran Phu Street. There was a new bridge across the river, so we turned left, then pulled over to a very recognizable building, and who was sitting out front watching the traffic pass by but my old friend. The cab pulled over and let us out. For a moment Emerson looked up but said nothing. He then jumped to his feet and walked over slowly to see if his memory was correct.

"I don't believe it" he said. "Ed Winslow. How the hell are you. Never thought I'd see you back in this town. And hello to you too Wales. Let's grab a seat outside here and I'll clue you in on Da Nang. And you Winslow can fill me in on your life. What'll it be, tea or beer?"

It's a hot afternoon, so we opt for beer. Things sure look different down along the river. The old docks are gone as is the fishing fleet. It resembles the river walk in San Antonio, with pavers between the street and the water way which is lined with an iron fence. They are sure making progress. I mention that to Wales.

"You can credit your old friend Van Ly with that," he says. "And this is just frosting. Look around at the buildings. Look across the river where the shore was once lined with slums. From what I've seen she's the most forward-thinking mayor or politician in Viet Nam."

I'd never forgotten that night we'd spent together so many years ago. That momentary relief and escape from impending death…for both of us. And the sexual ecstasy. It's lasted until, well today.

Fitz comes out with the beer, then starts in with his same old theme. "I've been here fifteen years and am just getting started cleaning up the mess you guys made of this country. It seems hopeless sometimes. And to top it off you threw twenty years of sanctions on top of the twenty year war. The 'sorest losers in the history of warfare' does not half begin to describe that great country of ours."

Wales had a smile on his face, "I'm aware it's not funny but let it go Fitz. This is a new age. Your country is beginning to be the biggest trading partner with its old enemy here. It's coming around. Be positive."

You could say I agreed with both of them. Things were bad, real bad and now they were looking pretty good, in fact real good. The hell with the past. Even my dear Lien.

"I'll tell you what," said Wales. "Let me call Van Ly and see if she has time for a quick get together with you."

"You can do that," I asked.

"I'm the fucking ambassador from the great USA, of course I can do that. We work together for god's sake."

He rang her up. Talked for a few minutes then relayed her message to me, saying that he'd have to pass on the visit. He had matters to catch up with Fitz.

"She'll meet you at the coffee shop behind the University of Da Nang building back up the street in twenty minutes. Start walking now and you'll be just on time. It's the tall building on the left. You can't miss it."

So I take off at a fast walk in spite of the heat, wondering as I move along just how this is going to go down. No way I could guess. And no way I could miss the building, the tallest in this part of the city. The coffee shop, which is half full of students is in the rear. And there sat my old and dear friend, my secret sexual partner Van Ly, the beauty from the Bamboo bar from so many years ago.

And she looks great. And ever more beautiful. Vietnamese women look young until they look old, and she sure as hell didn't look old. We didn't hug or nuzzle cheeks. Just a friendly handshake and a sit down.

"You look wonderful Van Ly," I said.

She looks at me in a curious way, smiles and says nothing. Of course, I'm wondering if she is going over in her mind our last moments together.

"It does seem like so many years ago my Captain…and of course it is. I've had such a time since then that I can barely recall my years at the Bamboo with my dear friend Lien. Not to leave out 'the boys' of course. No, it is great to see you, Edward Winslow. It's wonderful to see you. We parted after all in a great hurry. You to the South and me to the North….as it should have been, don't you think?"

"Perhaps we should let all of that go Van Ly. What about now, and you in this job. What about your family."

Before she answered I inform her of Lien's passing a couple of years ago, and she extends her condolences before continuing with her story.

"As you might have guessed my Captain, I had a husband from 'before'…if you get my drift."

Obviously, she still had a command of the old GI lingo, and I smiled thinking about it.

"Who can say old friend? It crossed my mind…but in the end I wasn't sure."

"You mean us that time," she said. "That be war. Sometime anything can happen and can be good. That is how we survived. And we did didn't we? I am now the mayor of this great city with a kind husband and four children. And I am happy. I could not ask for more."

We continue with that friendly talk for a time, but Van Ly isn't able to stay long, for she has meetings with the University people. After she leaves, I order another iced coffee and look over the college girls, just like the old days. But not for long. A slow walk brings me back to the offices of Rebuild Vietnam where Fitz and Wales are still out front talking over more cold beers. I went inside and said hello to Chi then brought one out for myself and sat down with them. They both look at me and smile.

"What did you expect," Fitz asks, "What did you find?"

Not being sure what he's driving at I say that I had found an old friend and we had a wonderful visit and I had a nice walk back here.

"What else Mr. Fitz."

"Nothing Ed, just bugging you. She's something isn't she."

I had to agree, and I might add so did Wales, the ambassador to her country.

"For me she's one of my best contacts in Viet Nam. Eventually I'll be able to be a greater help to Da Nang, and that will be because of my relationship with her and who she is. More officials like her and you'd see this country take off."

I was thinking that perhaps the US embargo of twenty years might have had something to do with why this country hadn't taken off faster, and mention that to Wales.

"Good point Winslow, but that's in the past. We're on it now."

"And it's about time," said Fitz. "Twice the tonnage of World War II then twenty years of enforced economic isolation. We're a great country we are."

"Isn't it about time we head off to the airport," I interject, hoping to change the subject.

"Let me finish," said Fitz. "I worked here for ten years before the embargo was ended and to say things were tight doesn't touch it. Any way... fuck it. You guys get going and have a safe trip back. No doubt we'll be continuing this conversation, somewhere, sometime."

With that Wales and I board a taxi for the airport and in less than two hours we're back talking with Mai at the Metropole bar over strong vodka tonics and lime. Somehow in Asia that's where everyone eventually ends up. It's either the heat or the women. And in this bar, at this time it's the woman, that's becoming obvious.

"How do you expect to pull this off being the Ambassador and all," I ask him.

"We're just friends Wales, just friends. No law against that is there."

Once again I figure to change the subject and let everyone run their own life. "What about Peters and Everest," I ask Wales. "You ever run into either of them."

"Everest I have, back in DC a couple of times. He's retired now but ended up being the CO of Seal Team Six. Pretty successful guy. You'd be interested in knowing that back in the day he left Da Nang swimming. Stripped down to his od shorts on My Khe beach and swam out to a navy boat that was picking up local escapees from small craft. They dropped him off on one of the carriers and he caught a flight back to Saigon a few days later. Not Peters. Nothing on him."

I mentioned that I had visited Len Peters last summer over on the Cape. He had been back in the States for some time, having spent a good ten years earlier being quite a respected English Teacher in Saigon, rather Ho Chi Minh City. It seemed like at this point he was staying put, enjoying the weather…and of course the Scotch.

"I can't be working all night here serving you two. Everyone else has gone home," said Mai as she pulled up a stool across from us. "Let's pack it in boys. I have to be at MK eight o'clock sharp in the morning."

"Please Mai, one last pour of Courvoisier and I will head up to my room. You and Wales can figure the rest out."

She smiled and said nothing but did eventually come across with that one last 'good pour'. I was becoming lost in thought about where I'd go now and mentioned that to my friends.

"You have no choice but to return to Thai Nguyen for another visit with Hoa. You can learn more about Lien and her life in Thai Nguyen before she moved to Da Nang. Maybe be friends with Hoa"

That was Mai's take and the more I thought about it, it would be mine too.

"Good night you two. I'm off to my room."

By eight the next morning I was in my newfound friend Quan's taxi on the road to Thai Nguyen. It was a nice morning starting out with warm sun visible for a change and no wind. Quite pleasant driving North from Hanoi toward the unexpected. Hell, I had no idea what I was doing or where I expected this trip to end but at least I wasn't standing still. I had no way to notify Hoa that I was coming for a visit but was hoping she was home. If not, I'd take a tour around the countryside of Thai Nguyen.

"When you go home?" asked Quan as we drove along.

"Maybe soon. I don't know yet, but I have no reason to hurry. I have all the time in the world."

"Lucky for you," said Quan. "I must work all day every day to keep me and family fed. That be it. No dreams no more…too old."

I tried to cheer him up. There's always hope I said, but he questioned that line of thought. Silence ensued till we pulled up to Hoa's place. I had his card and told him I'd give him a ring from Hoa's phone when I needed to be picked up.

"Don't worry about the price Quan, I'll pay you for the day…with a bonus."

He grinned as I stepped from the car and told him to wait a minute in case Hoa wasn't there before he left for his friend's coffee shop where I figured he'd be spending a good part of the day. Well….she is there and immediately invites me in for tea.

"So good to see you again my brother Edward. What brings you this way?"

I smile for a moment, then say "you, of course. I so much enjoyed our last visit."

She points me towards the back porch of her house which overlooked open land, while busying herself fixing tea. I began thinking of the past when Lien and Hoa were young girls helping their father farm this land and when she served us both tea it seemed that she was reading my mind.

"Lien and I loved working with my father in these fields" she said. "We rode the back of our water buffalo who was part of the family. He lived right beside our house…right back there," as she pointed to the other side which was now garden".

"Tell me about your lover who never returned," I asked. "When did you give up hope?"

"I haven't." she replied. "One never knows how the world will turn. If he walked across those fields towards us at this moment I would not be surprised. I'd expect it."

This led me to wonder if this girl, woman actually, was based in reality. It's been many years since the war's end.

She looked at me and smiled. "That's a fantasy my friend. I do know the real world."

She talked on about those times when her family was young, during the years between the French and American wars. Her father had fought at Dien Bien Phu but had made it home by mid '55. There were some tough years before the new government in the North figured things out but eventually they were living a peaceful life till the American war began.

I briefly skim over my life in Da Nang with Lien before the fall but find no need to dwell on the 'Bamboo'. It didn't seem relevant. We continue with our visit into the late afternoon, so I eventually call my faithful driver and ask him to hang in there, maybe stay the night if he didn't hear from me.

Hoa wants to take a walk so we tramp through her family fields, small by my standards from the farm country I'd known in my youth in Northern New York. The great difference here in Viet Nam is that the family graves are in the fields, generations of them. I mean perhaps back to Genghis Khan's time in some instances. And she has stories of all these relatives. It is near dark when we return to the house. Hoa fixes a charcoal fire and I fill her in more thoroughly on her sister's life with me in Australia. She eventually begins talking of her long lost lover Chanh, who had fathered her son. The fact that he had the same name as my captor back in the day meant not much to me since it is such a common name in Viet Nam.

"My last correspondence with Chanh was a letter he'd written before the Fall of Saigon that arrived here months later. He was thoroughly disillusioned with the war and his life in it. He said he'd be home soon, one way or the other. And that was the end. Not another word."

She begins sobbing then, and I try to comfort her.

"Would you have any cognac Hoa," I asked thinking that would change the mood.

"Of course," she replied, coming around. "I picked up the habit on a trip to Paris. We have always maintained a touch of French Culture up here in the North. French bread and cognac we keep. Just no more Dien Bien Phu's."

She serves a fresh baguette along with the Courvoisier, then begins rummaging through papers and old photos on her desk.

"Here Ed Winslow is a picture of my love Chanh. It was taken on his last trip home. You can see that we both appear so happy in this photo. I've never been there since."

I look over the photo and can't believe my eyes. It is the same Chanh that had been my captor, the same Chanh that had probably saved my life. Who knows what would have happened if he'd sent me back to the rear in those days? We have a long discussion about him after that fact had become known. Hoa wants to know everything about my time with her Chanh... everything. I would be the last personal contact that she would ever have with him.

I didn't stay the night but made plans to meet up with her in two days in Hanoi. She would look me up at the Metropole where I would be till departing later in the week. Let's face it, I was in no rush. I had nowhere to go that mattered.

As it turns out, the next night it's back at the bar, with Mai and Wales.

"So," said Wales, "sounds to me like you're going to take up with her."

"You must be crazy. I just met her...and she's my sister."

"Are you crazy? " he comes back with, "She is not your sister. In some cultures when a mate dies, they always remarry a sibling. That's the proper way."

"Mai, could you get us another round please. Make mine a double." I was back on the vodka tonic for a change.

"I think" said Mai as she served us, "you'd better look up this woman and get to know her better and see where it goes. That be rather like your friend Wales and me. Is that not correct my good friend Wales?"

He looked at me and smiled. "Yes, that is correct, my good friend Mai. That is absolutely correct."

Mai leaves to take care of other patrons at the bar and Wales begins talking of what his future might look like.

"I'm leaving my wife of twenty five years and retiring from the Foreign Service. They'd be letting me go, at any rate when it becomes known that I've left my wife for a girl in her twenties. A native girl no less."

I told him he was crazy. His family, his career… it would be too much.

"Like hell," he fired back. "You know what really matters Ed…food and fucking and of course good wine. And I'm with Mai. And the hell with the food."

I laughed to myself. "Go for it man. I understand. I'm seeing Hoa tomorrow and we'll see where things go".

I spend the next day with Hoa walking around Hanoi, and talking about everything under the sun. I can't recall a more pleasant time. We part with the understanding that I'll be back soon.

"Do not forget me," I ask of her.

She smiles at me… that beautiful Asian smile and says, "Never happen GI… never happen."

THE END